"My lips are sealed,"
Sam said.

"I know nothing about the fact that you are going to ask one of my two best friends in the world, Carrie Alden, to marry you. Even if I burst from excitement, your secret is safe with me."

"You?" Billy commented, groaning slightly. *"Sam Bridges, Sunset Island's walking gossip column, sworn to secrecy? What was I thinking?"*

"Just tell me this," Sam said. *"When are you going to ask her?"*

"I told you, I haven't decided yet."

"Haven't decided if or haven't decided when?" Kurt asked.

"Well, you've only got five days left," Pres reminded him. *"That's all any of us have."*

The room was silent.

Five days, *Sam thought.* Five days left in the greatest summer of my life.

Sunset Forever

CHERIE BENNETT

Sunset™ Island

SPLASH™

A BERKLEY / SPLASH BOOK

SUNSET FOREVER is an original publication of
The Berkley Publishing Group.
This work has never appeared before in book form.

"You've Got a Home With Me," by Jeff Gottesfeld and Joel
Emerson. Used by permission. Copyright © 1996 by
Jeff Gottesfeld and Joel Emerson. All rights reserved.

SUNSET FOREVER

A Berkley Book / published by arrangement with
General Licensing Company, Inc.

PRINTING HISTORY
Berkley edition / June 1997

A GLC BOOK

Splash and *Sunset Island* are trademarks belonging to
General Licensing Company, Inc.

The Putnam Berkley World Wide Web site address is
http://www.berkley.com

ISBN: 0-425-15765-2

BERKLEY®
Berkley Books are published by The Berkley Publishing Group,
200 Madison Avenue, New York, New York 10016.
BERKLEY and the "B" design
are trademarks belonging to Berkley Publishing Corporation.

PRINTED IN THE UNITED STATES OF AMERICA

10 9 8 7 6 5 4 3 2 1

As always, for Jeff, a fan
of the endless summer

And while I wish I could take credit for dreaming up the idea of the MORP dance, credit needs to go to Sunset sister Heather Justice, of Beaver Falls, Pennsylvania, who told me about it in a letter. Thanks, Heather!

ONE

"Oh, Billy, let's leave this island and run away together, right now, right this minute! Some place where no one can ever find us—"

"Your dialogue is a little stilted, Carrie, dearest," Billy Sampson teased. "You sound like a really bad movie."

"*Moi?*"

"Carrie, be serious," Billy insisted, his gorgeous dark eyes glistening in the bright early afternoon sunlight as it filtered through the window. "Because I've never felt more serious in my life."

"I'll try."

Billy dropped to one knee and looked up expectantly. He'd never seemed more nervous. "Carrie, I . . ."

"Yes, Billy?"

"Carrie, I want this more than anything else in the whole world," Billy said.

"Yes?"

1

"Carrie Alden, will you . . . will you marry me?" Billy asked, his voice cracking on the word *marry*.

"Would I *what?*"

"Marry me," Billy repeated, his voice dropping until it was a barely audible whisper. "Marry me. Be my wife. I want you to be my wife. Forever."

"Yuck! Blech! Are you kidding? Forget it!" Samantha Bridges yelled at Billy, shaking her head so violently that her long, luxurious red hair whipped the sides of her face. "Carrie says, out of the question! Married to you? Puh-leeze!"

"That's not what Carrie would say," Billy pointed out dryly. "You're supposed to be helping me rehearse my proposal, and it's supposed to be realistic—"

"Hey, I'm playing Carrie, not you," Sam said. "And I'm the professional actress, so I get to make up Carrie's lines, and she says: 'Gag me!'"

Presley Travis and Kurt Ackerman, who were watching Billy and Sam's big scene, cracked up. Pres was Billy's bandmate and Sam's on-again, off-again, currently on-again boyfriend. And Kurt was their good friend and Emma Cresswell's guy.

"Thanks for the support," Billy said to Sam archly. "You're a big help."

"Pardner, I told you this wasn't a good idea," Pres said to Billy in his easy Tennessee drawl as

2

he tied his long hair back in a ponytail. "This ain't like playing tennis. You can't practice marriage proposals on someone else."

"How do you know?" Billy challenged. "Have you ever made one?"

"No, but Kurt has," Pres replied, giving Kurt a wink. "Right, my man?"

Kurt buried his handsome face in his hands in mock emotional agony.

"I think Kurt's gonna take a big fat pass on that one," Sam observed. "His one and only marriage proposal didn't exactly turn out happily ever after."

"Emma and I weren't ready," Kurt said with dignity, finally taking his hands away from his face.

"You ready now?" Sam asked, wiggling her eyebrows at him.

"None of your business," Kurt told her with a grin.

"Aw, come on, no one's proposing to me! At least I can hear about it when it happens to my best friends!"

"Well, the answer to your question is no," Kurt said. "Emma and I still aren't ready."

"Too bad," Sam replied. "I was imagining this double wedding with Carrie and Billy—"

"Hey! You just told me Carrie is going to turn me down!" Billy reminded her.

"What do you think I am, a mind reader?" Sam asked. "How do I know what Carrie will really say?" She plopped down on the shabby couch and reached for the open bag of potato chips on the end table.

"Just remember," Billy told her, "you are sworn to secrecy. Not a word about this to Carrie until I actually get up the nerve to ask her, okay?"

"My lips are sealed," Sam said as she stuffed her mouth with an oversize handful of chips. "I know nothing about the fact that you are going to ask one of my two best friends in the entire world, Carrie Alden, to marry you. Even if I burst from excitement, your secret is safe with me."

"You?" Billy commented, groaning slightly. "Sam Bridges, Sunset Island's walking gossip column, sworn to secrecy? What was I thinking?"

"I'll keep my mouth shut," Sam promised solemnly. "As long as Pres and Kurt do, too."

"I must have lost my mind to practice a proposal with you," Billy said, shaking his head and picking up the cold bottle of soda he'd set down.

"Just tell me this," Sam said. "When are you going to ask her?"

"I told you, I haven't decided yet."

"Haven't decided *if* or haven't decided *when?*" Kurt asked.

"Both, I guess," Billy said.

4

"Well, you've only got five days left," Pres reminded him. "That's all any of us have."

The room was silent.

Five days, Sam thought. *Five days left in the greatest summer of my life.*

"I don't want to think about it," Sam said. "It's too depressing."

"The summer, over," Kurt said sadly. He glanced at the Greenpeace wall calendar. It was Tuesday, August twenty-sixth. "Hard to believe."

"It's been an awesome summer," Pres said.

Sam sighed. "The most fun I ever had in my life."

"Not all fun," Billy allowed. "What with Sly and all."

"Fun and hard," Pres agreed.

The living room of the house that Pres and Billy shared with the other two members of their band, Flirting With Danger, fell silent, as all four friends quietly contemplated the amazing two summers they'd spent together on fabulous Sunset Island.

All around them on the living room walls were mementos and photographs taken from the summer. Posters from the Flirts' recently concluded tour of Maine, where they'd finally been assured by Polimar Records that they were going to get their recording contract. An article clipped from the *Breakers,* Sunset Island's newspaper, about the Miss Sunset Island contest, in which

5

Sam competed. And there were many, many photos that Carrie had taken, of her and Billy together, Pres and Sam together, Kurt and Emma together, and of the band performing.

And a smiling photo of Sly Smith, the Flirts' original drummer, who had died from AIDS-related complications just a few weeks before. In the photo Sly was healthy—radiant, even—behind his drum kit, drumsticks in his hands. Now Sly was dead and buried, his memorial service a tortured memory.

What happened to Sly is horrible, Sam thought. *I still can't believe he's dead. Right before he died, he told me he wanted us all to be happy. And I am happy, or I would be if the greatest summer of my life wasn't about to end. But now what? Now what?*

Sam thought back on the strange and wonderful circumstances that had brought her, a nineteen-year-old girl from tiny Junction, Kansas, back to Sunset Island, the famous resort island in Casco Bay off the coast of Maine, for her second straight summer.

Sam had actually first come to Sunset Island the previous summer, when she'd been hired to work as an au pair—a live-in nanny—for Dan Jacobs, a single father who had two sometimes-hilarious, sometimes-obnoxious twin daughters, Becky and Allie.

The job was tough and the twins were more

than a handful, and Sam had even been fired once. But once Dan saw what life was like without her around, Sam had been hired back in a hurry.

It wasn't the job with the Jacobses that made Sunset Island so incredible. It was that Sam had become best friends with two other girls she'd met at the International Au Pair Convention in New York City—Carrie Alden and Emma Cresswell.

The Three Musketeers, Sam thought wryly. *That's us. The Three Totally Bizarro Musketeers.*

Never in a zillion years would Sam have figured that she'd end up best friends with Carrie—a girl who went to Yale, wanted to be a photojournalist, and whose parents were both pediatricians in New Jersey, and Emma—an actual Boston heiress whose family was one of the richest in America and who was studying French at Goucher College in Maryland.

Not that Emma is actually rich anymore, Sam reminded herself, *'cuz she isn't. Her mother took away all her money because Emma wouldn't drop Kurt as a boyfriend. I thought Emma would fall apart without her millions, but she hasn't. You just never know.*

The three of them had been best friends for more than a year now. And while Sam sometimes felt envious of Emma's background and Carrie's perfect home life, the two of them were just as envious of Sam's tall, slim looks, her ability to come up with hilarious one-liners and her creative fashion sense.

We even look totally different from each other, Sam thought. *Emma's petite and blond and loves to wear white, while Carrie's brunette and curvy— well, she thinks too curvy—and is sort of your basic girl-next-door. Of course, Carrie's the only one of us three who isn't a virgin—not that anyone would guess I was. But I am.*

Big joke. The world's biggest flirt is all bark and no bite, she thought to herself wryly.

The three girls not only had each other, but also had met great guys. While Emma had experienced some pretty bumpy times with Kurt, who was a native of Sunset Island, the two of them now seemed happier than ever.

And Carrie and Billy—they're practically married. No wonder Billy's practicing his proposal. As for me and Pres, well, who knows. First I'm chasing him, then he's chasing me. Sometimes I think I'm just not ready for a real relationship with him, and other times I think that he's so wonderful that I'm afraid of loving him and then losing him.

But in five days I'll be leaving him. Leaving everything.

What am I going to do with my life now?

"Too many questions," Billy said, finally breaking the silence.

"What do you mean?" Kurt asked.

Billy reached for his acoustic guitar, and started finger-picking absentmindedly on it. "What's gonna happen with Polimar? What's gonna happen with me and Car? And you and Emma? And Sam and you, Pres?" Billy looked at Pres.

"Who knows?" Pres said with a shrug. He picked a minor melody on his guitar. "It'll all work out."

"If Polimar doesn't call us in the next five days," Billy said darkly, "I'm gonna hit the roof."

"They promised," Sam reminded Billy as she took a sip of iced tea and reached for another handful of chips. "I was there."

"Yeah, right."

"Hey," Kurt suggested, "no sense moping here. Let's go to the beach."

Sam grimaced. "Can't," she said. "Now that summer camp's done at the club, I gotta take the twins to a Zit People practice."

Sam was referring to the industrial band formed by Ian Templeton, one of Carrie's charges, who also happened to be the son of rock star Graham Perry. The band had originally been called Lord Whitehead and the Zit People, but the name had been changed when Becky and Allie Jacobs became back-up singers for the band.

"Well, Play Café then, tonight," Kurt said, mentioning their favorite hangout on the island. "Ten o'clock. I know for a fact that Emma and Carrie have the night off."

"Cool," Sam said. "Billy can ask Carrie then, and we can all watch and go 'aw-w-w-w!'"

Billy answered by tossing a throw pillow at Sam, which hit her squarely in the face.

"Hey!" Sam cried out. "You want me to keep my mouth shut, right? Treat me nicely!"

Pres laughed, and then Kurt laughed, and then Billy joined in. And finally Sam broke down in laughter, too.

I don't know what I'm laughing about, she thought, even as gales of laughter filled the room. *Five more days and the summer's over.*

And I have absolutely no idea what I'm going to do with my life.

"Emma, I suck at Tetris," eleven-year-old Wills Hewitt said to Emma Cresswell as she walked into the Hewitts' family room, which housed the family's computer.

"Stink," Emma corrected automatically. "I stink at Tetris."

"Whatever," Wills mumbled as his small fingers flew across the arrow buttons on the computer, trying to maneuver the assorted falling shapes on the Tetris game into neat rows and thus rack up points. "I'm still terrible. Even Katie can beat me."

"Ha!" five-year-old Katie cried from where she was sitting on the couch watching MTV with the remote control in her hand. "I'm the best!"

"You are not!" Wills shouted, his eyes still on the computer game. "Emma's the best."

"Is not!" Katie shouted. "I am!"

Emma sighed. It seemed to her that during the past two days, as they all headed into the final week of the summer, Katie and Wills were fighting about anything and everything. And the volume level of their arguments was steadily increasing, too. At least their older brother, Ethan, was visiting his grandparents in Connecticut for a few days. One less kid to fight with.

"Look," Emma said, exasperated, "why don't we forget about Tetris for a while, and after dinner we'll play a different game together?"

"Okay!" Wills pronounced, his eyes still firmly on the computer monitor.

"Katie?" Emma asked.

"Uh-huh," Katie mumbled. She was now completely preoccupied by a video on the television set.

The phone rang. Emma picked it up.

"Hewitt residence, Emma Cresswell speaking," Emma said as she had answered countless times before.

"Emma! Honey!"

It's my father, Emma realized as she heard the familiar voice.

Emma's dad, Brent Cresswell, had become a lot closer to Emma over the past couple of years.

11

When he'd had a heart attack right on the Club Sunset Island golf course during a visit to the island, it was Emma who was at the Maine Medical Center every single day. And even though he'd lost a great deal of money in the recent stock market slide, he'd told Emma that he would try to get his estranged wife, Katerina "Kat" Cresswell, to lift the restrictions that she'd placed on Emma's own finances.

For the first time in my life, this summer, Emma thought, *I've been poor. And I've hated it. But I also found out I can live without my family's money, if it means that I get to run my own life.*

All in all, though, she admitted to herself, *it's better to be rich.*

"Daddy!" Emma replied. "Hold on a sec." She put her hand over the receiver.

"It's my dad," she said to Katie and Wills. "Can you two promise no fighting for at least fifteen minutes? I'd like to talk to him in my room."

Wills put the Tetris game he was playing on "hold." "I'll keep the brat in line," Wills said.

"I'm not a brat! You're a brat!"

"You guys!" Emma pleaded.

"Okay, okay," Wills said. "I'll hang up the phone down here."

"Okay," Katie said, her eyes glued to MTV.

Emma hustled to her room on the top floor of the expansive summer house, where she picked

12

up the phone from the nightstand. She heard Wills hang up the other extension.

"Daddy?"

"Emma, I'm so glad you're home," her father said. "Hold on, I'm patching in your mother."

My mother? Emma wondered. *Whatever for?*

"Darling!" Kat Cresswell said. "So nice to speak to you. What a treat!"

"Hello, Mother," Emma said, careful to keep her voice even. *I wonder if she forgot that she cut me off from the family fortune. You'd never know it from the tone of her voice.*

"Well, isn't it fantastic, darling?" Kat cried into the phone dramatically. "As you can see, your father and I are talking to each other."

"I can see that," Emma said, sitting down on her bed.

Kat laughed. "Even more than that," she pronounced slyly and gave a girlish little giggle.

Emma winced. So many things that her mother said or did made her teeth hurt.

"What is it, Mother?" Emma asked, wondering what the reason was for the call. Neither her mother nor her father called her up often just to chitchat.

"Well, your father and I were just talking about your future," Kat continued.

"This morning, at breakfast," Brent added.

"You're planning to go back to Goucher, right?" Kat asked. "In a few days?"

Emma looked around her room. She had already started to pack up some boxes.

"Yes," Emma said carefully. "That is, if my tuition is pa—"

Kat laughed. "Your tuition? Don't worry. It's paid, of course."

"You paid it?" Emma asked. "I wish you had told me—"

"Emma," Brent said, "your mother just said that your tuition has been paid. In full, might I add."

"But I thought—"

"Listen, darling," Kat said, "if you're at Goucher, you're not going to be with that silly boy, what's his name again? Burt?"

"You know very well his name is Kurt," Emma said. "Kurt Ackerman. And he's not silly."

"Of course," Kat replied. "I forgot. Anyway, if you're at school, you won't be with him. So why shouldn't you go to school?"

"School's important," Brent agreed. "I made that point to your mother, and she agreed with me."

"You know how persuasive your father can be," Kat added coyly. "I never have been able to resist him!"

Right, Emma thought. *That you divorced him*

and were planning to marry a sleazy artist who is closer to my age than yours shouldn't enter into the picture at all.

Emma took a deep breath. "I appreciate that you paid my tuition—" Emma began.

"And you'll need money to live on at school," her father said, "so we've unfrozen your trust."

"You've *what?*"

"We've unfrozen your assets, Emma, and it will take both our signatures to freeze them again," Brent said. "We figure that with your mother and I living together again, and with you at Goucher, we'll be able to keep a close watch on you. So why should you suffer?"

"Why should anyone suffer?" Kat asked gaily. "After all, we're Cresswells! Of course, you're only going to get the income from the trust; the millions won't be yours for a while yet. But you'll have an income of two hundred thousand dollars per year or so."

"Can you live on that?" Brent asked, chuckling.

"You're . . . the two of you are giving me back my money?"

"We just said that," Kat intoned. "The proper response would be 'thank you.'"

"Honey," Brent said, "will you need me to drive you to Goucher?"

"We could both drive her, dear," Kat told her ex. "That is, if we're in the country. But I suppose we could arrange to be in the country if you need us, Emma."

Emma was dumbfounded.

My parents are together again? And they're giving me back at least some of my money? I can't believe I'm having this conversation. Am I dreaming?

"Emma?" Brent asked.

"I'll, uh, call you," Emma said. "Later. Tomorrow."

"Just make sure that boy doesn't drive you to college," Kat said.

"Now, Kat, don't start on her—" Brent warned his ex-wife.

"What did I say?" Kat asked her husband innocently. "Just remember," she told her daughter, "some boys are fine for a summer fling, but then it's time to return to reality—"

"Reality," Emma echoed dully. She looked at her half-packed boxes. When she'd awakened that morning, she wasn't even sure she was going to be able to go to college that fall. She'd applied for financial aid, but Goucher seemed very skeptical that Emma Cresswell, of the Boston Cresswell family, was actually in need of scholarship help.

Now, just like that, her money problems were over.

I have no idea what reality is, Emma realized.

"So, ta-ta, sweetie," Kat sang out. "We'll talk to you later in the week. Hugs and kisses!"

"Take care, princess," her father added, and they hung up.

Emma leaned back on her bed and closed her eyes. She took five deep breaths.

I'm not dreaming, she thought. *I just had that conversation.*

But what if they find out that I'm seeing Kurt while I'm at Goucher, or writing him or calling him or . . .

I could be right back where I was this morning. Only worse.

Because I wouldn't have a job, or a place to live, either.

And then I have no idea at all what I would do.

TWO

Carrie stared up at the starry sky, one hand resting languidly in the sand. She could hear the waves crashing on the shoreline. Billy leaned over her, his lips meeting hers. She wrapped her arms around him, and—

"Yo, Carrie." Fourteen-year-old Ian Templeton called up the basement steps to where Carrie was sitting, pulling her out of her reverie about her date with Billy the night before.

The perfect evening, Carrie thought, *the most fantastic, wonderful—*

"Hey, Car, are you listening to me?" Ian asked impatiently. "I want you to check out our new song!"

"I'm checking it, I'm checking it," Carrie said good-naturedly as she leaned back on her elbows, resting them on the basement step.

I wish it were last night all over again. And I had my earplugs, Carrie thought wryly. *Here comes the aural onslaught.*

"Hey, Zits, let's rock it!" Ian shouted to his band. "Places!"

Sam had brought Becky and Allie Jacobs over to the Templeton mansion for their Zit People rehearsal.

Ian Templeton spent a lot of time in his father's awesome shadow, Sam and Carrie agreed.

They also agreed that, for the most part, the Zits redefined popular music.

And the new definition was, in a word, "awful."

At that moment Sam was in the bathroom, which left Carrie to face the Zits' tune all by herself.

I hope Sam gets back here soon, Carrie thought ironically. *Because I know she absolutely, positively doesn't want to miss the last rehearsal of the Zits' summer season.*

Carrie watched, bemused, as the five other members of Lord Whitehead and the Zit People, who'd been huddled together in a tight circle, singing the words *Hoo-hoo-hoo-hoo,* over and over (Ian believed that it helped center their energy, while Carrie found that it gave her the urge to flee from the room screaming) ran to their appointed places behind their individual "instruments."

Becky and Allie are backup singers with the Zits again, Carrie noted, seeing the twins position themselves. *They've been in, and out, and in. It all depends on how Becky's feeling about Ian that week.*

"A-one, two, three, FOW!" Ian yelled loudly, as if he were John Lennon or Paul McCartney shouting out the introduction to the Beatles' classic "I Saw Her Standing There."

Then he flipped a switch on a cassette player, and the actual Beatles version of "I Saw Her Standing There" began pouring out of the massive tower speakers Ian's father had installed in his son's basement "studio."

Band members Marcus Woods and Donald Zuckerman started pounding on a derelict microwave oven and a washing machine, respectively, with long iron pipes, while William "The Refrigerator" Kerry repeatedly slammed another long iron pipe into a retired Whirlpool refrigerator that had been turned on its side.

Meanwhile, the twins chanted the word *seventeen* over and over again, into their stand-up mike. And then Ian, who stood center stage in front of another stand-up mike, began to snarl into it:

> "Come hither, my sweet Rosalind
> 'Tis long since thou and I have met;
> And yet methinks it were unkind
> Those moments to forget."

"What's *that*?" Sam shouted in Carrie's ear over the intense racket of the Zits.

Carrie turned to her friend. "P. B. Shelley, I think!" she yelled. "Ian's reciting the beginning of *Rosalind and Helen*."

"What?" Sam yelled. "Shelly who?"

Carrie held her hands up to her friend, realizing that conversation was futile until the Zits' "song" finished. Which it did a minute or so later, with Ian reciting more lines from the famous poem, and the Refrigerator pounding out a particularly syncopated rhythm on the Whirlpool's defunct ice maker.

"Whoa," Ian said solemnly, when the song was over.

"Whoa," Becky and Allie added.

"Whoa," Donald and Marcus said, practically simultaneously.

William the Refrigerator didn't say anything. He just gave a couple of extra smashes with his iron pipe to the Whirlpool, as a kind of percussive punctuation mark.

"Heavy," Ian pronounced, and all the band members nodded in agreement.

"You think we can slip out of here?" Sam asked Carrie quietly. "I could use an aspirin."

"Uh, Ian," Carrie said to the bandleader, "we've got to go upstairs to, uh, think about how brilliant that song was."

"You really think it was brilliant?" Ian asked Carrie, his eyes shining.

"Brilliant," Sam answered for Carrie. "More than brilliant. Beyond brilliant."

"Thanks," Ian said self-consciously. "We've only been working on it for a day."

Sam tugged gently on Carrie's shoulder. "Carry on, you musical dudes," she said. "We'll be right upstairs. Contemplating."

A few moments later Sam and Carrie were sitting in the Templetons' family room on one of the plush leather couches. They were surrounded by wall plaques, gold and platinum records, and all the other various awards Graham had won during his long and distinguished rock-and-roll career. A bowl of grapes rested between the girls. The Zits had plunged into another tune, but fortunately the basement was soundproofed.

Mostly.

"What was that poet's name?" Sam asked as she settled into the couch.

"Shelley," Carrie repeated. "P. B. Shelley. Famous romantic."

"Like Shelly Plotkin," Sam mused, grinning. "Famous romantic."

Shelly Plotkin was the too-enthusiastic, balding artist-and-repertoire guy that Polimar Records had sent to scout the Flirts before they were finally offered their recording contract.

"Can you imagine having sex with Shelly Plotkin?" Sam asked, popping a grape in her mouth.

"No," Carrie replied.

"Me, neither," Sam said with a shudder. "I think about stuff like that all the time. Like, I look at really conservatively dressed people, and I think: Do they have sex? But a lot of times these people have kids, which means they had to have sex, so then I try to picture—"

"Your mind is a thing of wonder," Carrie interrupted.

"Oh, yeah," Sam agreed. "Thanks."

The "music" from the Zits escalated, and Sam put her hands over her ears. "I'm going to miss the Zits," she said.

"Right, I'll bet," Carrie said, laughing.

"Ya never know," Sam said. She reached for a grape and flipped it up in the air, then caught it expertly in her mouth as it fell.

"No, you're not," Carrie said, trying the same thing with a grape that Sam had done. The grape bounced off her chin, rolled down her throat, and disappeared inside her men's white V-neck T-shirt, buried somewhere in her cleavage.

"What's it like to have a cleavage?" Sam asked.

"What's it like to be skinny enough to wear a bikini?" Carrie countered.

Sam shrugged. "It's just normal to me. Hey, you might want to save that lucky grape for Billy—"

"Sam!"

"Sorry," Sam said meekly.

"I don't even know if I'm going to see Billy after Labor Day." Carrie sighed as she picked the grape out of her shirt and put it on the table.

"You haven't talked about it?" Sam asked her, honestly surprised.

I am dying to tell her that Billy is actually thinking about proposing marriage to her, but I gave my word that I wouldn't, Sam reminded herself.

Carrie nodded her head. "We talk. Too much, sometimes it seems."

"So," Sam prompted her friend, "tell the Great Redheaded One everything you've been yakking about."

"The Great Redheaded One?" Carrie joshed.

"Just a nickname," Sam assured her. "I sort of like it."

"Well, don't you ever feel that you can talk *too* much?" Carrie asked. "Like, do you and Pres ever talk so much with each other that you end up knowing less than when you started?"

"No," Sam said blithely. "Never happens. He distracts me in other . . . more distracting ways."

"It happens with Billy and me," Carrie said, sighing slowly.

"You don't cut him off by covering him with kisses from head to toe?" Sam joshed.

Carrie took another grape. "This is serious, Sam."

"I *am* serious."

"Sam," Carrie said, "you might not know what you're going to do on Monday, and that might be okay with you, but I know exactly what I'm going to do."

"Which is what?" Sam asked, picking up another grape and tossing it into her mouth.

"Go back to Yale," Carrie said. "Register for classes. Start my sophomore year."

"Well, you've got it wrong about me," Sam said lightly.

"You've decided—"

"Yup," Sam said. "I know exactly what I'm going to do."

"Amazing," Carrie said, turning to her friend. "I thought you'd never decide."

"I'm going right back to Junction, Kansas, where I'll eat myself into oblivion," Sam intoned seriously, "gain about a hundred pounds on a diet of stale Doritos, and go to work as a cashier in a pharmacy."

"But—"

"Oh, yeah. Becky and Allie are going to be my au pairs, because I plan to have triplets," Sam concluded.

Carrie laughed, and Sam did too. Earlier that summer Sam had had a terrible nightmare, where she'd dreamed exactly what she just told Carrie.

"No, seriously," Carrie said, "what are you going to do?"

"Who knows?" Sam asked blithely.

"You don't have long to figure it out," Carrie pointed out.

"Five days," Sam retorted. "That's plenty of time for some rich guy to fall in love with me and take me away on his yacht forever."

"You don't want that," Carrie noted.

"I don't know," Sam said. "I could try it for a while before I reject the idea completely—"

"Come on," Carrie said. "I know you better than that. Really. What are you going to do?"

Sam reached for another grape. "I wish it were as easy for me as it is for you," she said. "You go back to Yale, stay in Yale, graduate from Yale, and then get a job taking pictures for *Time* magazine or something. But that's not me."

"What is you?" Carrie pressed.

Sam shrugged. "Fame and fortune, of course!"

"Seriously—"

"Seriously," Sam said. She was quiet for a moment. "Beats me. Maybe we could trade places, and you could figure it out for me."

Carrie sighed. "Everything isn't so easy for me, either. I mean, I'm going back to Yale, Billy and the band are going to be under contract to Polimar—"

"They haven't actually gotten the contract yet," Sam reminded Carrie.

Carrie dismissed her with a wave of the hand. "Someone called Billy from Polimar about an hour ago."

Sam leaned forward eagerly. "And you didn't tell me? What did they say?"

"That the record contract's being sent to them by overnight express mail," Carrie said. "It'll be at their house tomorrow."

"That's fantastic!" Sam cried. "That's incredible! It's taken forever!"

Carrie leaned back on the couch. "I tell myself it's fantastic," she confessed, "but what it also means is that Billy and I won't . . ."

Her voice trailed off despondently.

"Well," Sam intoned, "maybe Billy has other ideas."

"I don't think so," Carrie said. "The Flirts mean everything to him. Why should I hold him to a higher standard than he holds me?"

"You mean—"

"Exactly," Carrie said emphatically.

Earlier in the summer, when Billy's father had suffered a devastating accident, Carrie had gone back to Seattle with Billy to see him. Billy had wanted them both to stay in Seattle to take care of his dad, but Carrie, after taking a searching look at her own life, had decided that her own future was more important, and she returned to the island. Fortunately, Billy's older brother was able to stay in Seattle instead of Billy, so Billy had come back to the island, too.

"If I wouldn't stay in Seattle for Billy," Carrie reasoned, "why should I expect Billy to give up the band to come with me?"

Sam thought about it, and thought about it, but she didn't have a very good answer.

In fact, she didn't have an answer at all.

THREE

"Dang but that was a good time last night," Pres drawled as he poured himself another cup of coffee—jet black, as he always drank it.

"Agreed," Billy said. "Play Café, Carrie, Emma, Sam, Kurt, great tunes on the jukebox, can't ask for anything more, can you?"

"Another two weeks on the island, maybe," Pres said with a rueful smile.

"You got me there. Right back 'atcha," Billy agreed. "Right back 'atcha."

Billy glanced at the cheap white plastic clock on the kitchen wall, the one that always seemed to tilt slightly to the right no matter how many times they'd straightened it.

"Ten-twenty," he said. "Federal Express ads say they guarantee delivery by ten-thirty in the morning. That is, if Polimar really sent it."

"They sent it," Pres drawled. "Don't you worry, pardner. They sent it. Too bad Jake and Jay aren't here."

Jake Fisher was the band's drummer who had come into the band when Sly had developed full-blown AIDS, and Jay Bailey had long been the band's keyboard player. Both of them were out of town visiting Jay's family until the next day.

"And Sly," Billy reminded Pres. "Don't forget Sly."

"How could I?" Pres asked.

"Where is it?" Billy asked nervously, pacing back and forth across their small kitchen.

"You're gonna wear out the linoleum, man," Pres said, sipping his coffee.

"It was already worn out when we rented this place," Billy pointed out. He went to take a bite of a buttered bagel and then put the bagel back down on his plate. "Am I kidding? I'm too nervous to eat anything."

"They sent the contract," Pres repeated again.

Billy just looked at him. *How can he be so calm when I'm so nervous?* he wondered. *We've both waited so long for this, and he acts like it's just another day on the island.*

"You want some coffee?" Pres offered.

"Oh, yeah, caffeine, that's just what I need," Billy said sarcastically. "I'm jumping out of my skin as it is—"

"Take a cold shower or meditate or something," Pres suggested.

"How can you be so calm, man?" Billy asked.

"'Cuz I have faith," Pres said. "Polimar said the contract is coming and I believe that it's—"

"So where—"

Ding-dong.

The old-fashioned doorbell on the Flirts' house sounded.

Billy felt as if he could actually hear the pounding of his heart.

"Right there, big guy." Pres grinned. "Now, you go and get it."

Billy couldn't contain his enthusiasm. He practically ran to the front door, opened it, signed the receipt where the delivery guy said that he should sign, and then took the thick big envelope from him, turned, and loped back to the kitchen.

He dropped the envelope on the table. The sender's name, Polimar Records, was clearly visible on the front label.

"This is it," Billy said.

"Yeah," Pres agreed.

They both stared at the envelope.

"Well, we should enjoy it," Billy decided. He ran his hand nervously through his thick, dark hair. "Our first major label contract. It only happens once."

Pres clapped him on the shoulder. "I'm enjoying it," he told his longtime partner. "Now, let's open the thing and read it."

"You do the honors," Billy said, shoving the white envelope at Pres. "You're a month older than me."

"Forget it," Pres said, shoving the envelope back at Billy. "You're practically dying here."

"Okay," Billy said as he ripped open the pull tab and extracted three sets of legal-looking papers.

"One for you, one for me, one for the lawyers," Pres quipped.

"Shut up and read," Billy growled, handing one of the sets of papers to Pres.

For a moment or two Billy and Pres had their heads buried in the contracts.

"There's a mistake," Billy muttered as he peered down at the second page.

"How do you figure?" Pres said, looking up at his bandmate, who had already read several paragraphs ahead of him.

"Jeez!" Billy shouted, suddenly flinging the contract across the kitchen so that it slapped against the far wall and then slid messily to the yellowed linoleum floor.

"Hey, chill," Pres advised him. "What'd you read in there?"

"They're screwing us!" Billy shouted. "The damn company's—"

"But—"

"Pres, this isn't a recording contract!" Billy thundered. "This is a song-writing publishing contract!"

"Well," Pres said reasonably, "someone just made a mistake."

"We'll see," Billy said darkly, going for the kitchen telephone. "Go get your butt on the other extension. I'm calling Leete. Right now."

Leete—Cody Leete—was the business-suited, conservative-looking Polimar executive who had flown in from New York to see the end of the Flirts' last concert mini-tour of Maine. Leete was the one who'd told them, at the end of that concert, that the band was going to be offered a record deal.

Pres went into the living room, picked up the cordless phone in there, and brought it back into the kitchen. By the time he pushed the On button, Billy was already dialing Polimar in New York.

This had better be a mistake, Billy thought as the call went through. *This had better be—*

"Polimar Records," a smooth female voice answered.

"Cody Leete," Billy snapped into the phone. "Tell him it's Billy Sampson."

"One moment, please."

"I'm gonna kill this guy if he did this on purpose," Billy told Pres.

"Don't get all bent out of shape until we know more," Pres advised him.

Pres and Billy stayed on hold for a while, and

then Leete's familiar, somewhat formal-sounding voice spoke up. "Cody Leete."

"Cody," Billy said from between gritted teeth. "It's Billy Sampson and Presley Travis. From Flirting With Danger in Maine."

"Hello, fellas," Leete said. "The contract arrived safely?"

"Yessir," Pres chimed in. "But it's a song-publishing contract, not a recording contract."

"That's right," Leete said. "We've had an opportunity to discuss your band here at corporate, and we've decided we want to take the two of you in a different direction."

"But—" Billy began to speak.

"Listen," Leete said, "the two of you are fine songwriting talents. Together, especially. 'Love Junkie' is a great, killer tune."

"Thanks," Pres said.

"But we just don't think the market is right now for your band at this time," Leete added.

"Let me make sure I understand this," Billy said, his voice low and tense. "You want us to *write songs* for you? You don't want the band? After all we did to prove ourselves to you?"

"Let me point out that it's a staff writing deal," Leete said. "You both get a retainer. A retainer is—"

"I know what a retainer is," Billy spat into the

phone. "You're throwing some money at us so we can write songs only for you. But what about the rest of my band? What about them?"

"It's the two of you we're signing," Leete said succinctly. "The others are good musicians. I'm sure they'll get other gigs."

"Other gigs," Billy repeated. "Other gigs. That's all you think the Flirts are, just one damned gig?"

Pres shot Billy a look that told him to chill out, but he was too livid to care.

"I understand that this is a surprise," Leete intoned, "but it's really a terrific opportunity for the two of you, Billy and Pres."

"Listen, Cody, opportune this," Billy said, then slammed the phone down as hard as he could.

I don't believe he just did that, Pres thought, shocked. "Hello? Cody?" he said into the phone. "Are you still there?"

"I'm here," Leete replied. "It sounds as if your partner there is a little upset."

"You could say that," Pres agreed, looking at Billy, who was staring down at the contract in his hands as if he could set fire to it with his eyes. "He's, uh, he's a passionate guy."

"I like that," Leete said. "But I don't want any loose cannons in the Polimar family."

"He's not a loose cannon; he just cares about his art," Pres said, his Tennessee accent thickening as it always did when he was under stress.

"He's calling me a loose cannon?!" Billy yelled. "That lying jackass? He's the one who's—"

Pres silenced him with a wave of his hand, and Billy shook his head in abject disgust.

"Look, Pres, just read through the contract and talk it over," Leete suggested. "I don't need to point out that thousands of songwriters in the country would kill to get the break I've just handed to the two of you. You want to do the deal, we're ready to do it with you two. Okay?"

"Okay," Pres replied, his eyes imploring Billy to remain silent. "We'll call you later in the week."

"You do that," Leete said, and then he hung up the phone without saying good-bye.

Pres turned the phone off and set it down hard on the table.

"That scum-sucking, low-life pile of—" Billy began.

"Have you lost it, man?" Pres asked. "Are you out of your mind, insulting Cody Leete like that?"

"Is *he* out of *his* mind?" Billy snorted. "Sending us a damned music publishing contract? Without any warning? Music publishing?" There was unconcealed venom in his voice.

Pres reached for his now-lukewarm coffee. "Look, let's read the contract over and talk about this. All I'm saying is don't let's jump to conclusions."

"Is that what you call it?" Billy asked. "He just pulled a fast one on us, get it?"

"Plenty of great performers got their careers started as songwriters," Pres pointed out.

"Country music," Billy sneered. "Country performers."

"Rock and country," Pres countered. "Both."

"We're performers," Billy said, his voice full of steel. "I want a performing contract, not a songwriter's contract where we're writing songs for someone else to get famous on."

"Hold on, man—" Pres began.

"What do you mean, 'hold on'? They promised us a performing deal; that's what we're gonna get."

Pres scratched his chin. "Wait, you mean you're fixing to turn this down? Without even thinking about it?"

"I'm not 'fixin' to,'" Billy replied. "Because in my mind, it's already turned down."

"But—"

"Pres," Billy said, his voice rising, "we have not played in two-bit dives all over the country for the last three years so that we can get a songwriting contract from a record company that told us they were giving us a recording contract!"

Billy, who rarely used profanity, then colorfully cursed Polimar Records in general, and Cody Leete in particular.

Pres just stared at him, not sure what to do. *I've never seen Billy like this before,* he realized. *And I don't know how to get through to him before he throws everything away.*

"Billy," Pres said slowly, "you need to calm down and think about this some."

"Why?" Billy said. "They're screwing us. We should just take it?"

"What else do you suggest we do?" Pres asked.

"Turn it down, that's what I suggest we do!" Billy said angrily.

"Just like that," Pres said.

"Yeah, just like that," Billy echoed.

"And then what?"

"Then we get our asses back on the road like we always do. I want my dad in Seattle to turn on the TV sometime, see you and me on that screen, and say, 'Hey, that's my boy.'"

Pres whistled. "So that's what this is all about." He took a sip of his cold coffee. "I get it."

"Get what?" Billy asked.

"I get what's goin' on with you now. This isn't about music, or your career, it's about bein' on TV."

"You're full of it," Billy shot back.

"It's about bein' on TV so you can prove something to your old man," Pres continued.

"You don't know what you're talkin' about," Billy said, flustered.

"You just figure that your family, who are against this whole music thing anyway, won't be impressed with no songwriting deal," Pres said. "But a recording deal, CDs with your name on them . . . that, they get."

"It isn't like that," Billy said.

"Yeah, it is," Pres said. He looked Billy in the eye. "This isn't about what's best for us. You haven't even considered that yet. It's about what's gonna impress your family."

"That's bull," Billy said, but the heat came to his face, and his voice was defensive. "What about our band, huh? What do you think we're gonna tell the other guys, that we got a sweet deal and they can go to hell? I care about my friends. And I'm not a sellout. Unlike someone in this room."

"You take that back," Pres said, stung.

"The truth hurts, huh, Pres?" Billy taunted him. "You just want the easy way out. You're a quitter, man."

Pres laughed coldly. "Me, a quitter? I want to quit, I can go back to Tennessee, go to Nashville, and do session work anytime I want. You're the one who's dreaming, buddy boy. I'm a realist."

"And here I thought you were an artist," Billy said coldly. "Guess I was wrong."

"What do you think this is, Billy, some danged movie?" Pres yelled. "This is real life. The real thing. We don't get to call do-over! And we can't just make Polimar do what we want!"

Billy stared Pres down. "Let me explain this to you slowly so you can understand. I've worked my butt off for years to get a recording deal. So have you. I thought that's what we both wanted. So let's take this piece of crap and send it where it belongs. Down the toilet."

"Bad idea, bro," Pres said.

"Come on!" Billy pleaded. "I'm willing to do anything I have to do to get that recording deal. Aren't you?"

"If the road to getting a recording contract goes through this songwriting contract, I'm signing this thing quicker than white gets on rice," Pres said.

"And what about Jay and Jake?" Billy asked.

"Like I said, if this deal leads to a recording deal, then we're all in it together. We don't sign this, we're throwing it all away."

"Bull," Billy said. "You're signing nothing."

"Since when do you get to tell me what to do?" Pres reached for a pen that was lying on the table.

But Billy was quicker. He took the Polimar contract that was in front of Pres, held it in front of himself, and tore it in half, length-wise. Then he tore it in half in the other direction. Then, he let the ripped pieces of the contract flutter from his hands down to the kitchen table.

"You're crazy," Pres said.

"Yeah, I am," Billy agreed. "Crazy for believing all these years that you were the guy I thought you were. But you're not. You're nothing but a quitter, man. A lousy, two-bit quitter."

Pres felt as if Billy had punched him.

"Go to hell, Billy," Pres said. He pushed his chair back so hard that it fell over. "Go take a rocket straight to hell." He stormed out of the kitchen, leaving Billy contemplating the torn-up contract in front of him.

What did I do? Billy thought. *What did I just do?*

But his best friend was gone, and no one was there to comfort his broken heart.

FOUR

"The beach, the beach, the beach!" Sam sang out lustily in an impromptu song as she strode through the open front screen door into the Hewitts' house and down the hallway into the kitchen, Carrie trailing a few feet behind her. "How I love the beach!"

"I never would have guessed," Carrie teased.

"Hey, Emma-bo-bemma, you ready to fry in the hot sun on the hot beach in a hot bathing suit?" Sam asked her friend.

Emma was in the kitchen, serving a snack of muffins and fruit to Katie and Wills. Their parents, lawyers Jane and Jeff Hewitt, were sitting with them drinking lemonade.

Emma looked at the wall clock.

11:59.

All three girls looked at each other.

Just a few minutes earlier, Pres and Billy had had their terrible fight, but the girls knew nothing

45

about it yet. Instead, they were thinking about the time.

Exactly one more minute, Emma thought to herself. *All of our contracts with our families run through noontime today. In one more minute Carrie and Sam and I will be free women. It'll all be over. But our contracts say that we can continue to live with our host families until September 1.*

No more work. I can't believe it.

And I can't believe the summer is ending, either. It seemed as if it was never going to happen.

Slowly the hands of the clock slid to noon.

"That's it," Carrie said. "It's noon."

"How do you all feel?" Jane Hewitt asked them.

"I don't know," Carrie said honestly. "I really don't."

"Well, I know how I feel," Sam said. "Liberated! Carrie does, too, even if she doesn't realize it yet."

"What she means," Carrie said slyly, "is that Graham and Claudia gave me the rest of the day off after ten-thirty this morning. Which means I have the rest of the year off, I guess."

"Now Dan gets to enjoy his twins all by himself," Sam chortled happily. "Good luck!"

"Well, congrats to all of you," Jeff Hewitt said. "You guys did a great job."

"Especially you, Emma," Jane said warmly. "Although I suppose I'm biased."

Emma blushed. "Thanks, Jane," she managed. Katie dropped her spoon, and Emma hurried to get her a clean one.

"Hey, you don't have to do that anymore!" Wills said. "Your job ended!"

"Habit," Emma said, handing Katie a clean spoon.

Wills drilled his finger into his muffin. "I guess you were only nice to us because you were getting paid," he said sadly.

Emma put her arms around the little boy. "Wills, I was nice to you because I like you so much."

Wills blushed happily. "Better than Ethan?"

"I like all of you," Emma said.

"A born diplomat," Jane said with a laugh.

"And too terrific to lose," Jeff added. "Which leads me to ask, can you come back next summer?"

Sam, Emma, and Carrie just looked at one another.

Next summer? Emma thought. *This one isn't even over yet. I can't bear for this to be over. . . .*

"I'm not sure—" Emma began.

"Jeff," Jane interrupted, "let's let Emma enjoy her last few days here before she goes back to college, without worrying about next year."

"Sorry," Jeff said sheepishly. "I just wanted to get early dibs on you."

"Oh, that's okay," Sam said. "Dan Jacobs asked me the same question."

"And Graham and Claudia asked me the same thing too," Carrie added.

Jane and Jeff laughed. "It's nice to be popular, huh?" Jane said.

"What did you two say?" Emma asked her friends.

"Same as you," Carrie said, shrugging. "Who knows what happens between now and then?"

"I can't even figure next *week* out yet," Sam added.

Jane smiled. "I remember what it was like to feel that way. Enjoy it. Once you hit thirty and turn into a parent, you end up planning years in advance. And time goes by so fast sometimes it feels as if life is on fast-forward."

"Thirty?" Sam echoed. "I'll never be thirty."

"What's the alternative?" Carrie asked her.

"Well, Emma," Jeff said, "I just want you to know that the entire Hewitt family loves you. And if you want your job back next summer, you know what to do and who to call."

"Thanks," Emma said softly, her eyes misting involuntarily. She loved Jane and Jeff almost as if they were her own parents, and had hardly had any disagreements with them during the two summers she'd worked for them.

Unlike Sam and Dan or Carrie and the Temple-

tons, she thought. *Jane and Jeff are the nicest, wisest, most understanding adults I've ever met in my life. Their kids don't know how lucky they are to have them as parents.*

"You're going to the beach?" Katie Hewitt asked Emma, her eyes growing wide.

"As of right now, Emma is a free woman," Jane told her daughter.

Katie's eyes got even wider. "She doesn't have to be with me anymore?"

Emma hugged Katie. "I'll still spend time with you, as long as I'm here. I promise."

"Good!" Katie cried. "I'll get my bathing suit!"

Everyone laughed.

"Not right now, little one," her father said, lifting Katie high into the air. "Emma has plans with her friends."

"But I'm her friend," Katie said. "Right, Emma?"

"You are definitely my friend," Emma assured her.

Jeff kissed his little girl's cheek. "I meant she's going out with Carrie and Sam."

"Are you sure it's okay if I go now?" Emma asked Jeff. "If there's anything you need—"

"Emma, sweetie," Jane said with a smile. "Read my lips: You're free."

"Okay," Emma replied. "Then I'll see you at dinnertime."

"Emma," Jane said gently, "you don't have to have dinner with us tonight if you don't want to."

"I want to," Emma said earnestly, and all four Hewitts at the table beamed with undisguised pleasure.

Emma and her friends walked out of the house into the blazing noontime sun.

"Lez-go-a-beach," Sam sang out, throwing her arms wide. "I mean, I've picked the perfect lez-go-a-beach uni, don't you think?" She spun around so that her friends could check out her latest outfit: She wore a tiny bikini covered with Disney characters, and over that a transparent beach cover-up that didn't cover anything up, and transparent plastic sandals on her feet.

"I know you used to dance at Disney World," Carrie said. "But I never saw that bathing suit before."

"I mail-ordered it from a Disney catalog," Sam confessed. "Want me to order one for you?"

Carrie laughed and looked down at herself in her usual conservative navy-and-white one-piece bathing suit, with the bra built in for extra support. "I would get arrested in that bathing suit."

"Okay, then, you, Em," Sam coaxed. "Just once I'd like to see you in clothing with a sense of humor!"

Emma had on white shorts and a tiny white

T-shirt over her white bathing suit with the mesh inserts and high-cut legs. She had bought the bathing suit before her money had gotten cut off—it was from a very expensive South American designer.

I have to tell them that my parents gave me my money back, Emma realized. *I don't know why I didn't say anything yet. I guess I feel kind of funny, making such a big deal about money, when both of them live on such tight budgets all the time.*

"Hey, I have an idea!" Carrie said as they headed for the car she had borrowed from the Templetons. "Let's stop by and see if Erin can come with us!"

Erin Kane was, along with Sam and Emma, a backup singer for the Flirts. This was Erin's first summer on the island, and the girls had become great friends with her. She had fabulous long, curly blond hair, a gorgeous face, and an even more gorgeous singing voice. She was also fifty pounds or so overweight, and Sam could not get over the fact that Jake, the Flirts' drummer, was dating her, or that so many guys seemed to be attracted to her.

"She left for New York this morning to audition for some band," Emma explained. "She called me last night."

The Flirts had officially decided that at the end of the summer they would no longer have back-up singers, which left Erin to look for other vocal work.

Erin is so good she should be a lead singer instead of a back-up singer, anyway, Emma thought. *Backup singing was just a lark for me. I suppose Sam is the only one of the three of us who will really miss being a part of the Flirts.*

"Will Erin be back before we leave the island?" Carrie asked.

"She said she'd try to, but if she gets this gig she has to start rehearsing with the band right away," Emma explained. "Anyway, she promised me she'd come visit all of us, wherever we end up. And we can always contact her through her parents, she said."

"I'll miss her," Carrie said softly.

"Me, too," Sam said. She got into the car and slammed the door. "I hate this. Erin is the first one of the group to split. Soon everyone will leave. Soon it'll all be over."

For a long while Carrie and Emma didn't say anything. What could they say? Sam was right.

Carrie started the car, then pulled into the street and headed for the beach.

"Let's just try to enjoy the time we have left," Emma said. "I don't want to spoil the last few days we have here by moping around."

"That's easy for you to say," Sam said. "You're going back to college. And so is Carrie."

"What about you?" Emma asked Sam.

"I'm living in the moment," Sam said firmly. "Tomorrow will just have to take care of itself."

"But what do you want to do?" Emma pressed.

"I don't know, okay?" Sam said, an edge to her voice.

"Don't get mad at me!" Emma said. "I wasn't trying to push you or anything."

"Emma just means that we only have a few days left before—" Carrie began.

"You guys, I know," Sam said. "I'm counting the hours, the minutes, the seconds, okay? Can I help it if I don't want to face it? Can I help it if I can't bear the thought of saying good-bye?"

Emma reached into the backseat and took Sam's hand. "I know," she said softly.

"Oh, I refuse to be sad!" Sam cried. "Let's head for the beach! Let's ride the waves, get a sunburn, break a few hearts! The summer isn't over yet!"

"Wow!" Sam said. "Look at that!"

Carrie and Emma, who'd been lying down on their beach towels, sat up and followed Sam's finger.

She was pointing to a perfectly bronzed guy standing at the edge of the water, who looked like he'd just stepped out of a bodybuilding magazine. He was incredibly muscled and perfectly chiseled, with long sandy hair down to the middle of his back.

"It's Fabio," Sam breathed, pointing the guy out to Emma and Carrie.

"That's not Fabio," Carrie said.

Sam dismissed her with a shake of her head. "Hey! Fabio! Yo!" she yelled out. "Over here!" She gesticulated wildly.

Fortunately the breeze coming in off the ocean prevented Sam's words from carrying to the guy.

"Sam, down girl," Carrie cautioned her friend. "Go jump in the ocean and cool off. Pres might meet us here later."

"He wouldn't be mad if I was talking to Fabio over there," Sam said. "I don't even like muscles that big. I'd be talking to him for research purposes."

"What's the research?" Emma asked.

"The research is: Could I get to like guys with muscles that big?" Sam said seriously.

Carrie and Emma laughed.

Sam swung her head around toward Carrie, momentarily taking her eyes off the guy. "Where are those binoculars?"

"Sam, you're incorrigible," Carrie said.

"What's that mean?"

"It means—"

Sam laughed. "I know what it means," she said, "'cause you've called me that before. I consider it a mark of honor or something." She found her binoculars and looked at the guy. "Poetry in motion, I mean it, you guys," she told her friends. She put the binoculars down. "I hate winter. A guy like that cannot be appreciated with too many layers of clothing on him."

Emma shook her head. "How would you like it if a guy talked about you like that?"

"Like what?" Sam asked.

"Like you were nothing more than a sex object," Carrie explained.

"Hey, I expect to be appreciated for my mind, okay?" Sam said. "But first impressions count."

"Let's talk about something else," Emma suggested, spreading some sunscreen down her legs. "Like what we're going to do for the rest of the summer."

"All four days of it," Carrie said with a sigh.

"I don't want to talk about it!" Sam cried. "It's too depressing!"

"Well, there's the guitar pull tonight at the Flirts' house," Carrie reminded them. "That should be fun."

The gang had decided to have what Pres called a "guitar pull" that evening, which he described as a Tennessee tradition where people got together with their musical instruments and went around the room singing and playing songs they had written. Pres had suggested that they have potluck desserts and then do the pull in the backyard, under the stars.

They invited a bunch of people, Carrie recalled. *It's going to be so much fun. . . .*

"Hey, did anyone call the guys to see if their contract came from Polimar?" Emma asked.

"Not yet," Carrie said, "but we can all celebrate tonight."

"And tomorrow night is the MORP party," Emma said, "that should be fun."

"MORP—PROM spelled backward," Sam said. "How cute."

"Any party up at the Masons' house is fun," Carrie said.

"And unique!" Emma added.

The Masons were Carolyn and Gomez Mason, who were horror-movie writers. They lived in a scary-looking mansion on top of the biggest hill on the island. They had a sixteen-year-old daughter, Molly, who had been crippled in a car accident the year before and was now confined to a wheelchair. Molly's best friend, who also lived with them, was Darcy Laken.

She's one of the most terrific girls I've ever met in my life, Emma thought. *She lives with the family so she can help the Masons with Molly. She grew up poor, but she never talks about it. And she's got ESP, though she doesn't seem to have any control over when she knows what's going to happen in the future, and when she doesn't.*

And she and Molly always throw incredible parties.

"That mansion they live in is out there," Sam said. "What a great place for a party!"

"Any party where you get to invite the guy is fun for you," Carrie joshed.

"Everything at the MORP is backward," Emma said. "Girls invite guys, everyone dresses down, all the decorations are cheap—"

"Works for you, huh, Em?" Sam cracked. "Now that you're an ex-heiress?"

"Actually, that's changed," Emma said slowly. She quickly explained the conversation she'd had with her parents.

"That's so terrific!" Carrie exclaimed. "I'm so happy for you! They're paying for school and everything?"

"Yes," Emma said.

"Are there strings? Like not seeing Kurt?" Carrie asked.

Emma sighed. "Not in so many words. I would never agree to that. But they're hoping that I'll be at college and he'll be far, far away. But I keep thinking that—"

"Wait, what you're saying is that you're rich again," Sam interrupted.

"I guess so," Emma agreed.

"Just like that," Sam said.

"Sam, come on—" Carrie began.

"No, it's cool," Sam said. "I'm happy for you, Em. I just wish I could get a phone call and be rich, just like that."

"Money isn't everything, Sam," Emma said.

"Funny how it's only people with money who say that," Sam quipped. She reached over and tickled Emma in the ribs. "Oh, don't worry, Em. I'm happy for you. And the MORP party is going to be a blast."

"It should be fun," Emma said with dignity.

"If everyone on this beach shows up," Sam noted, scanning the beach from end to end and taking in the sea of nearly bare bodies, "it's gonna be an amazing bash."

The beach was packed. The week leading into Labor Day was traditionally the busiest week of the year on Sunset Island, and every single hotel room, motel room, bed-and-breakfast, and campsite was occupied by people who'd flocked to the island from all over North America. Jane and Jeff Hewitt had described it to Emma as Homecoming Week, and it didn't seem as if that was very far from the truth.

Sam started making siren sounds. "Wooo-woooo."

"Now what, Sam?" Carrie asked her.

"Red alert! Red alert!" Sam intoned, faking the sound of radio static in her voice. "Two o'clock, coming this way. Load your rifles, ladies. Shoot when you see the whites of their eyes."

"What are you talking a—?" Emma began. And then she saw what Sam was referring to.

Diana De Witt. And Lorell Courtland. Their two archenemies. The nastiest two humans ever put on the planet.

"I don't believe it," Carrie said. "Is that Daphne with them?"

"I don't believe it, either," Emma said. "The last time I saw her, she tried to kill me."

Daphne Whittinger, who really had tried to kill Emma earlier in the summer in the midst of an insane rage, was walking between Diana and Lorell.

"Isn't she supposed to be in prison or a mental ward or permanent rehab or something?" Carrie asked.

"Maybe she got pardoned by the governor—" Emma speculated.

"To reform the three-headed She-Devil-From-Hell," Sam quipped, and the girls laughed.

Emma had gone to boarding school with Diana, but they'd never been friends. Diana and Lorell, since the girls had met them their first summer on the island, seemed to be on a mission to make the girls' lives miserable. The fact that they were gorgeous and knew it didn't make Sam, Emma, and Carrie's lives any easier. Diana had even seduced Kurt the summer before.

And I've never gotten over it, Emma thought to herself. *Not completely. Not really.*

"Hey, Diana," Lorell trilled in her sugary, southern accent as she, Diana, and Daphne approached the girls. "Look what the cat dragged in."

"Cat crap, I see," Diana said maliciously. Her friends laughed as if she had said something hilarious.

The gruesome threesome stood over Sam, Emma and Carrie. Diana lifted her sunglasses to look at the girls. "Well, I thought the last few days on the beach were going to be beautiful," she said sadly, "but evidently I was wrong."

"Bite me, Diana," Sam said.

"Oh, Sammie," Lorell cooed, "I am soooo wounded. Anyway, is that any way for a young lady to greet an old friend? Say hello to Daphne again, okay?"

Emma, Sam, and Carrie all muttered hellos.

"Daphne's out on a day pass," Diana confided, "Aren't you just overjoyed?"

"I'm afraid to ask where they usually have her locked up," Sam whispered to Emma. Emma nudged her in the ribs.

"It's nice to see you, Daphne," Carrie managed to say.

"I bet," Daphne said. She pushed some of her short, lank blond hair out of her eyes. She didn't look quite as awful as she did when she'd freaked out and tried to kill Emma, but she didn't look a whole lot better, either.

"So, Emma," Diana asked, plopping down on the girls' blanket uninvited, "what are you going to do when the summer's over?"

Emma didn't say anything.

Okay, she thought, *why shouldn't I answer her? I have nothing to be afraid of. She's just evil. And I'm not.*

"I'm going back to Goucher," Emma said evenly.

"And Kurt?" Diana asked.

"You know very well Kurt's starting back at the Air Force Academy," Carrie said, her dark eyes blazing.

"Oh, really?" Diana asked, her lips spreading in a malicious grin.

"Really," Emma said.

"Hey, Daphne," Diana asked, looking up at her friend. "Isn't the Air Force Academy in Colorado Springs?"

"Uh-huh," Daphne assented. "I read that some-place."

"It's in Colorado, all right," Lorell agreed.

"Well, what a coincidence!" Diana said gaily, letting some sand run through her fingers.

"What's a coincidence?" Sam demanded as Emma got an uneasy feeling in her stomach.

"That Colorado College is in Colorado Springs,

too!" Diana declared. "Because that's the school that I just transferred to!"

"What a coincidence!" Lorell trilled.

"An amazing coincidence," Daphne agreed.

Emma's face grew pale under her tan, and Carrie reached for her hand and squeezed it.

"Why don't you just go crawl back under the rock you came from, Diana?" Sam asked.

Diana got to her feet. "Gosh, I don't think that's a very good idea." She smiled maliciously at Emma. "I'd rather go to Colorado Springs. Where Kurt is."

"Go away," Emma said, her voice low. "Go away and leave me alone."

"Alone," Diana repeated. "Yes, I'd say that you're going to be alone very soon. Be sure to drop me and Kurt a note from college, telling us how you like it."

"No wonder everyone calls you Diana De Bitch," Sam spat at her.

"Oh, that," Diana said, laughing. She turned to her friends, who also laughed, then she looked back at Emma. "I told you I'd get him back. You should have listened to me." She leaned close to Emma. "Enjoy your last four days with Aqua Man," she said, using her nickname for Kurt. "Because after that, he's mine. And there's nothing you can do about it."

FIVE

"Your turn," Billy said tersely as he strummed a couple of quick, angry chords on his twelve-string guitar.

"Let me borrow your ax?" Pres asked, his voice a little cold. "I want to use the twelve-string." He got up from where he was sitting on the floor, his arm draped lovingly around Sam, and walked over to where Billy was sitting.

Wordlessly Billy took off the twelve-string and gave it to his bandmate. *Every time I look at him I feel betrayed all over again,* he thought sadly.

He gave Pres a cool look. "Why don't you play something that you've written?" he asked acidly. "You want to be a writer so much."

Pres just shrugged, took the guitar, and strapped it on.

Billy shook his head with disgust. *I don't even know who Pres is anymore,* he thought. *How could he sell the band out like that? How?*

The guitar pull at the Flirts' house was in progress. Pres had never showed up at the beach that afternoon—he had been too upset about his fight with Billy to think about hanging out in the sun. In fact, he'd nearly called the guitar pull off.

Word about their big argument had spread quickly among the friends. Billy had called Carrie and told her about it, and Pres had called Sam. Then both Sam and Carrie had called Emma, one after the other. And now they were all gathered in the Flirts' living room, just the same.

Emma looked over at Billy and winced at the anger etched on his face. *Kurt is the only one who doesn't know yet, since he ended up with a double shift driving his taxi. He'll be really upset when he finds out. The rest of us decided that no matter what the guys decided to do, we were not going to be drawn into it and end up taking sides.*

That's what we promised each other.

Now I hope that's what actually happens.

Emma glanced over at Carrie and then at Sam, who looked back at her and shrugged helplessly.

I can't believe that this fight is going to ruin our last days of the summer, she thought.

"You playing or not?" Billy snapped at Pres.

Pres just gave Billy a cool look and strummed a few soft chords.

It would have been a bigger gathering if Jake, Jay, and Erin hadn't been away from the island, but other friends were there to clap and sing along. There was Howie Lawrence, the son of a very rich record executive who had a summer house on the island; Molly Mason, who was dating Howie; and Darcy Laken with her boyfriend, Scott, who was an officer with the Sunset Island police department.

And now, it was almost over. They'd been passing around instruments and singing for a few hours. They'd gone through the Flirts' entire repertoire, after having munched on the desserts all of them had brought. Scott had to pull the 11 P.M. to 7 A.M. patrol shift, so the gang had agreed to end the pull in time for him to get to Sunset Island's tiny stationhouse and change into his patrol uniform.

"So, play something I've never heard before," Molly suggested eagerly. "Have you guys written any new songs lately?"

"Oh, sure," Pres said easily.

"Although we're not likely to write any more any time soon," Billy added pointedly.

Carrie, who sat next to Billy, put her hand softly on his knee. They had all agreed to be civil during the guitar pull, and so far they had kept their word.

"Actually, this is a tune I wrote without Billy," Pres said. "I've been working on it some lately—

never played it for anyone before, as a matter of fact."

"Let's hear it," Howie Lawrence encouraged, his arm draped around Molly.

Now he's writing songs and hiding them from me, Billy thought, a scowl on his face. He folded his arms angrily. *I hope it stinks.*

Pres did some quick finger-picking on the guitar, and then began singing.

> Dusk settled on the water, the evening
> star shined bright
> We reeled our baits up to the boat, in
> the still of the August night
> One last fishing trip together before I
> left for school
> I was full of youthful pride, Daddy shared
> with me this simple truth:
>
> Life can turn you inside out and upset
> your grandest plans
> Stand tall, work hard, and keep your faith
> Try to take it like a man
> But if the world has beat you down, and
> you got no place to be
> You don't have to be alone, you've got a
> home with me.

"That's fantastic!" Darcy gushed involuntarily, and then everyone shushed her as Pres finger-picked his way through a riff. He closed his eyes, his face a mask of intensity and emotion, as he began the second verse.

My home stood in perfect order, like any house
of cards
One day it came tumbling down,
who'd have dreamed it could be so hard?
Daddy drove down and picked me up,
got me back up on my feet,
shared again those gentle words,
and the promise that he'd swore he'd keep

Life can turn you inside out and upset
your grandest plans
Stand tall, work hard, and keep your faith
Try to take it like a man
But if the world has beat you down, and
you got no place to be
You don't have to be alone, you've got a
home with me.

Pres's refrain was so singable and so easy, and its sentiment was so heartwarming, that by the time he reached the second half of it, practically everyone in the room was singing along with him, some adding a simple harmony line. And then, the song took an unexpected twist.

After fifty-five years together, Momma gently
passed away
Daddy's health had long since failed, this
was all that he could say
I worked hard, stood tall, but I'm so scared
to be alone . . .

Pres's voice took a short pause, and his voice
seemed to catch in his throat as he sang the next
two lines.

So I took my daddy's hand, and I held it as
I brought him home.

Life can turn you inside out and upset
your grandest plans
Stand tall, work hard, and keep your faith
Try to take it like a man
But if the world has beat you down, and
you got no place to be
You don't have to be alone, you've got a
home with me.
You don't ever have to be alone, you've got
a home with me.

No one sang along with Pres on the final chorus,
they were all so moved. And no one cheered,
either. Sam was crying visibly, and Emma felt a
tear roll down her own cheek.

Of course, Emma thought. *Pres was adopted, too, just like Sam. Pres doesn't even know who his biological father is. It must have broken his heart to write that song. My mother and father might be impossible, but at least they didn't give me away—*

Emma looked over at Billy, who seemed to be struggling with himself. "That's a great song, man," he finally said. "Now, *that's* a song."

"Thanks," Pres said.

Their eyes met, and Pres's seemed to be asking Billy to understand.

But I can't, Billy thought. *He's willing to throw everything away and take the easy way out. When Jay and Jake hear about this, they're gonna go nuts. I tried to reach them at Jay's parents' house in Boston, but they had already left. And now I'm sure not looking forward to the fireworks that are gonna come down when they get back and hear that the Flirts are history.*

"Now that I know what a guitar pull is, I think we should have lots of them," Molly said.

"Next summer," Howie suggested, pulling Molly close.

She looked at him sadly. "Next summer is so far away."

"I know," he agreed.

The room grew quiet.

Pres played a few low, minor chords on the guitar. *Who knows where we'll all be next summer,* he thought. *Everything changes. Even my friendship with Billy. Everything moves on.*

"You guys, let's cut the long faces," Sam insisted. "This summer isn't over yet. Besides, we'll all be together next summer. We have to!"

"Yeah, next summer," Howie agreed as he stroked Molly's hair.

Next summer, Emma thought.

Who knows if there really is going to be a next summer?

Tick.

Tick.

Tick.

Emma bolted upright in bed, awakened by the odd noise.

What was that?

She took a quick look at the clock—it was two o'clock in the morning. After the guitar pull, she had met Kurt for a late cup of coffee at the Play Café, and then they had gone for a walk on the beach. Emma told Kurt everything that had happened between Billy and Pres. He was just as upset about it as she was.

Tick.

There's that sound again, Emma thought. *It's my window! Someone's throwing something up against the window of my room!*

Emma rushed to the window and looked down.

Standing there, prepared to throw still another pebble against Emma's window, was Kurt.

Just like he did at the beginning of last summer when we fell in love, Emma realized. *Just like he did that time we had such a terrible fight. Oh, I love him so much. . . .*

Emma hurriedly opened her window, and Kurt beckoned for her to come down. So Emma pulled on a pair of jeans and a T-shirt, and, as quietly as she could, so as not to wake anyone else sleeping in the Hewitt house, she tiptoed down the stairs and out the front door, then hurried into the backyard where Kurt was waiting.

She stepped into his arms, and he held her tight.

"We can't go on meeting like this," she teased him.

"I didn't want to wake everyone with a phone call," Kurt said gently. "But I had to see you."

"But we didn't have a fight," Emma replied. "Whenever you toss pebbles—"

"Do we have to have a fight for me to want to see you in the middle of the night?" Kurt asked.

Emma answered by kissing him, and Kurt returned the kiss. For a moment they clung to each other, their hearts beating as one.

"Let's walk and talk," Kurt suggested. "I have something I want to talk to you about."

Hand in hand, they walked down the deserted street.

"It's about the end of the summer," Kurt said, "about what's going to happen—"

"It's okay, Kurt," Emma said. "We'll write to each other every day, we can send E-mail, we can call each other—"

"It's not that," Kurt said hastily. "It's more than that."

Emma's heart jumped in her chest.

What could be more than that? she thought. *Is he going to dump me? No, that can't be, not after how he kissed me.*

Oh, God.

He's not going to ask me to marry him again, is he?

Oh, God.

But what Kurt actually said surprised Emma more than if he'd asked her to marry him for the second time.

"Emma, I'm . . . I'm quitting school," Kurt said softly.

"You're *what?*"

"Quitting school," Kurt repeated. "Leaving the Air Force Academy."

"But you can't do that!" Emma exclaimed. "Do you realize how many people would love to get into the Air Force Academy? How can you just—"

"I've made my decision," Kurt said firmly. "And

it's final. I'm going to try to get a leave of absence, but if they won't grant me one, I'm not going back."

Emma was stunned. She could not imagine Kurt, who had grown up poor on Sunset Island, whose mother was dead and whose father was a lobsterman, turning down the chance to go back to the Air Force Academy and then become a career officer in the United States Air Force.

And then Emma had a fleeting thought, a thought that both made her a little sick and gave her a big thrill.

It's me, she thought. *It's because of me. He wants to come to Maryland where I'm in school to be with me. My mother would absolutely kill me.*

And then Emma had another thought, a thought that gave her an even bigger thrill.

No matter where he goes, Diana De Witt is in for a huge surprise when she transfers to Colorado College and finds out that Kurt isn't in Colorado Springs.

Hah! Take that, Diana.

"So . . . what are you going to do?" Emma asked.

"Stay," Kurt said forthrightly.

Emma looked at him uncomprehendingly.

"I'm staying here," Kurt repeated. "Right here, on Sunset Island. Right through the off-season."

She stared at him, too shocked to speak. An owl

hooted in a tree. It was the only sound in the still, night sky.

"I know you're surprised," he finally said.

"That's a major understatement. What are you going to do?" she asked.

"Help Dad," Kurt answered. "Work for COPE."

COPE was the Citizens of Positive Ethics, a public-interest advocacy group on Sunset Island that was dedicated to helping the poorer people who lived year-round on the island, and to protecting the island's natural resources from sometimes-unscrupulous developers. Emma had done some volunteer work for COPE in the past, and she had a tremendous amount of respect for the organization.

"What does your dad think of this idea?" Emma asked, trying to get her own thoughts in order.

"He loves it," Kurt replied.

"Really?" Emma asked. "He doesn't mind that you're going to drop out of the academy?"

"Emma, my dad loves this island like . . . well, like it's another one of his kids. You know how much it means to him."

"I do," Emma admitted.

"He's perfectly fine with my decision," Kurt said. "So now the question is, what do you think?"

Emma took a deep breath.

What do I think? she asked herself. *I don't even know. I know he loves this island, but dropping out of school? It seems so final.*

"I can always go back to school later on, you know," Kurt said, as if reading her mind.

"But could you go back to the Air Force Academy?" Emma asked.

"I don't know," Kurt admitted. He stopped walking and turned to Emma, his arms around her waist. "But the academy was never my big dream in life. I hope that doesn't disappoint you—"

"No—" Emma said quickly.

"Good," Kurt said. "Because I would never want to disappoint you. This doesn't change a thing about us, you know," he said, his eyes glinting in the moonlight. "I'll come to visit you at Goucher, and you can come up to the island. It's so beautiful here in the winter."

"I know how much you love this island," Emma said. "It's your home."

"Someday," Kurt said, "maybe it will be your home, too." He kissed her softly, then she buried her head in his chest.

"It feels like my home, already." Emma laughed. "I feel as if I'm leaving home to go back to school."

"Well, remember Pres's song," Kurt said lightly. "You'll always have a home here on Sunset Island. You'll always have a home with me."

"Oh, Kurt," Emma said, tears stinging her eyes. "I don't want the summer to end."

His only answer was another kiss, which went on and on until Emma forgot everything but what it felt like to be young and so in love.

SIX

". . . and then he told me he was staying right here on Sunset Island, to work for COPE," Emma said as she twisted to and fro in front of the full-length mirror in Carrie's room, trying to see what she looked like.

"He's giving up the Air Force Academy?" Carrie asked. "Wow, I sure never expected him to do that."

"Me, neither," Emma admitted.

"Well, that makes three of us," Sam said as she lolled on Carrie's bed. "And he looks so cute in that uniform, too."

"The uniform is beside the point," Carrie told her.

"Fashion is never beside the point," Sam replied solemnly. She squinted at Emma. "And speaking of unis, the one you have on needs work."

Emma looked down at her white silk shift. "What's wrong with it?"

77

"According to Molly, this MORP thing is very casual," Carrie reminded her.

"I'm casual," Emma said defensively.

"Emma, you're wearing a designer original," Sam said dryly.

"Yes, but a *casual* designer original," Carrie pointed out, her voice teasing.

Emma turned to her friends, her hands on her hips. "Okay, what am I supposed to wear?"

"I know just the thing!" Sam exclaimed. She went into Carrie's closest and pulled out a long sleeveless lime green top made of stretchy spandex. She held it up. "Ta-da!"

"What am I supposed to do with Carrie's shirt?" Emma asked.

"On Carrie it is a shirt," Sam said. "On petite little you, it is called a dress." She thrust the garment at Emma.

"Oh, no," Emma said. "I do not wear lime green spandex." She handed the shirt back to Sam.

Sam shrugged. "Okay, I do." She looked at Carrie. "Can I wear it?"

"Sure," Carrie said. "You're the one who talked me into buying it in the first place. I've only worn it once, and even then I felt like an idiot."

Sam slipped out of her cutoffs and T-shirt, then pulled the top over her head. It ended just below her butt. "Perfect!" she cried, looking at herself in the mirror. She looked down at the red cowboy boots that were her trademark. "Lime green with red? What do you think?"

"It makes me shudder, frankly," Carrie said.

"Nah, I like it," Sam decided.

"Well, I'll stick with what I'm wearing," Emma decided. "Kurt loves this dress."

"You mean I'm the only one of the three of us going to this thing in jeans?" Carrie asked.

Emma sat down on the bed next to Carrie. "I have this bad feeling in my stomach. . . ."

"You're sick?" Carrie asked with concern.

"No, no, about Kurt," Emma said. "Do you think I should have tried to talk him into staying in school?"

"He's a big boy," Sam said. "He gets to make his own decisions. Anyway, school is highly over-rated."

"Spoken like a true dropout," Carrie said as she got up to get her hairbrush.

The MORP dance at the Masons' house on the hill was set for eight P.M., and the Masons had told everyone that they were planning to serve breakfast on the back porch at five A.M. the next morning, to anyone who cared to last through the night.

"I happen to have a huge future ahead of me," Sam said. "I just haven't figured out what it is yet."

Emma sighed and threw herself back on the bed, and stared up at the ceiling.

"What was that sigh for?" Carrie asked.

"I'm not sure," Emma said honestly. "I mean, it's one thing for me to be in school at Goucher while Kurt's at the Air Force Academy, but . . ."

Her voice trailed off.

"You're thinking it'll be weird for you to be in school and him not," Carrie surmised.

"She thinks if he's not in school, Kurt Ackerman might be thinking about something else," Sam said. "Or someone else."

"That's not true," Emma said, a little irritated.

"Not at all?" Sam asked. "Not even an eensy, teensy, little—"

"Okay," Emma said, "I'm guilty."

"Told ya," Sam said. "I can't wait to see the look on Diana's face when she finds out that her little plot to live in the same town as Kurt has failed!"

"I have to admit, I will enjoy that," Emma said. She got up and went to stare out the window, looking out onto the expansive grounds of Graham Perry's estate, and to the ocean beyond that.

"You don't have to worry about Kurt falling for someone else," Carrie told Emma. "He's truly crazy about you."

"Right," Emma said, still staring out the window.

"Why am I getting the feeling that something about all of this is still bothering you?" Carrie said.

"Carrie Alden, psychologist to the rich and famous," Sam quipped. "Now that Boston heiress Emma Cresswell is rich again—"

"I'm serious," Carrie interrupted Sam.

"It's just going to be odd, being in school," Emma said, "while Kurt's up here working for COPE."

"So why don't you work for COPE, too?" Sam asked blithely. "Car, can we scrounge up some junk food? Because I am starving here."

Emma turned to face her friends. "That's just what I was thinking," she said softly.

"What?" Sam asked, not understanding.

"Ever since I woke up this morning," Emma said slowly, "I've been thinking about Kurt. And the island. And COPE. Just what you said."

"I have absolutely no idea what you're talking about," Sam said. "Emma, you make less sense than Becky and Allie."

"Not going back to school," Emma explained, leaning against the windowsill. "I'm thinking about staying here on the island. Right here. Working for COPE. Just like Kurt. With Kurt."

Her two friends looked at each other in shock.

"Did you really just say what I think you really just said?" Sam asked.

Emma nodded.

"Did Kurt ask you to?" Carrie wondered.

"No," Emma admitted.

Sam laughed. "This is a joke, right?"

Emma walked back over to her friends and sat down on the bed. "No joke," she said quietly.

"Em, get a grip," Sam said. "Your parents just gave you your money back. Are you looking to lose it again like that?" She snapped her fingers to indicate how fast she thought Kat Cresswell would cut Emma off from her money once again if she thought that Emma was going to stay on the island with Kurt for the winter.

"It doesn't have to happen like that!" Emma said, color rising in her cheeks. "It doesn't!"

"But it will," Sam advised.

Silence. Both girls looked at Carrie, who was deep in thought.

"What do you think, Carrie?" Emma finally asked.

Carrie took a few strands of her long dark hair and twirled them absentmindedly before she finally answered softly.

"Where will you live? What will your parents think? What will Kurt think? And finally and most important of all, is it what you really, really want to do?" Carrie asked.

"I want to do this," Emma said. "I think."

"You'd better know," Carrie advised her. "Would you do this even if your parents cut you off again?"

"God, planning the future just sucks," Sam said.

"Why do we have to be so serious and plan every little thing out, can someone please tell me?"

Carrie's thoughts involuntarily jumped from Emma's problems to her own. *Here I am, giving Emma Cresswell advice about the future, when I should be advising me. I always assumed that I'd just go back to Yale, and Billy and Pres would tour with the band. But now, there might not even be a band! What's Billy going to do? And is it going to involve me?*

"I don't know how you can *not* plan your future," Emma told Sam.

"Hey, I'm just a 'live-in-the-moment' kind of babe," Sam quipped.

"Well, I guess I'm not," Emma said. "And . . . I know I want to do this."

"But do you want to do it because you want to be with Kurt or because you want to help people with COPE?" Carrie asked.

Emma looked down. "Both, I suppose," she said in a small voice.

Sam jumped up from the bed. "Well, all I have to say is, you'd better have a real blast tonight, Em. Because as soon as your mom finds out about your plans for the winter, you can kiss your life good-bye!"

"Par-tee!" Sam shouted at the top of her lungs as she and her friends piled out of the caravan of vehicles they'd driven to the Masons' spooky mansion on the hill.

There'd been no surprises about who was inviting whom to the MORP party. Sam had asked Pres, Carrie had asked Billy, and Emma had asked Kurt. And, despite the cold war that was going on just below the surface with Billy and Pres, all six of the friends had gotten together for pizza at the Play Café before caravanning together to the Masons'—Kurt and Emma in one of the taxis Kurt sometimes drove, Pres and Sam on Pres's motorcycle, and Billy and Carrie in a fatigue-green Humvee army vehicle that Graham Perry had purchased on a whim the week before.

It was a good thing that they arrived when they did—the super-long driveway leading up to the Masons' house was lined with all kinds of cars, and vehicles were parked every which way, even on the front lawn.

"When the Masons throw a party, they throw a good one," Carrie said. "Look, there's Molly!"

Molly was being pushed at top speed in her wheelchair around the front of the house by Howie Lawrence, and both of them were laughing hysterically.

"Maniac Mason," Emma said. "That's what Molly's nickname was before the accident."

"I hope Howie hasn't had any beer," Sam observed as the six of them approached the house.

"Why not?" Pres asked her.

"They could book him then for speeding and drunk driving," Sam said as the friends came to the spooky front door.

Usually, the imposing, black front door would be opened by Lurch, the Masons' lugubrious-looking butler. But tonight the door was wide open, and the sounds of a very wild and very fun party spilled out into the warm late-August night.

"Hey!" Billy shouted. "Look over there! Isn't that—nah, it can't be—"

Everyone looked to where Billy was pointing.

"I can't believe he would show his face on this island," Sam said.

"I knew the end of the summer was too good to be true," Carrie agreed.

"Maybe," Sam began, "I could sneak away before he sees—"

Too late.

Standing by one of the drink-and-food tables was none other than the world's sleaziest photographer, Flash Hathaway. He turned in their direction and gave a broad smile and a wave.

"He's actually waving at us?" Sam exclaimed. "As if we're supposed to be glad to see him?"

Carrie groaned. "He's coming this way."

Flash worked his way through the crowd, followed by a sycophantic-looking younger guy, his faithful assistant, Leonard Fuller.

Flash wore his usual outfit of a silk shirt open nearly to the navel, too much jewelry, white linen trousers, and white Capezios. Leonard, his assistant, had dressed for the MORP dance in plumber's blue coveralls over an unbuttoned loud Hawaiian shirt.

They both looked ridiculous.

The girls had met Flash and Leonard many times. Their first summer on the island, he'd taken sleazy lingerie photos of Sam and exhibited them without her knowing it. Then he'd been hired by *Rock On* magazine to take photos of one of the Flirts' tours. And then he did an advertising shoot in which Sam and Emma had been involved.

He's like a summer cold you can't get rid of, Sam thought suddenly. *Can't I just spray him with some wasp repellent once and for all?*

"Hey, Emma!" Leonard called out. "Wanna dance? I'm known for my dancing, remember?"

"Who could forget?" Emma called back to him.

He might be the worst dancer I've ever seen in action, Sam thought, stifling a laugh.

"So, you ready to boogie, babe?" Leonard asked Emma hopefully.

"No, thanks, Leonard," Emma said. "I'm . . . busy."

"Come on," Leonard urged her. "It's a great tune! And I could take a babe like you to the moon!"

86

Kurt laughed. The guy was clearly too ridiculous to take seriously.

"Leonard has come out of his shell since the last time you saw him," Flash told the group. "I've been helping him out with his social skills."

"Oh, good," Carrie managed, biting her lips to keep from laughing.

"I'll pass," Emma said evenly.

"If you'll excuse us," Kurt said, taking Emma's elbow.

"Hey, Ice Princess!" Flash called to Emma. "No need to walk away!"

"She's not walkin' away from you, Flash," Pres drawled.

"Yeah, she's crazy about me," Flash said. "Always has been."

"No," Pres continued. "She's *runnin'* away!"

"Hey, that's a joke," Leonard realized.

"But I thought I might get some end-of-summer action photos of all the girls," Flash said, fingering the camera that dangled around his neck. "And I do mean action, if you catch my drift. There's a nice deserted place where you can hang your clo—"

"Flash—" Carrie said. "Are there no depths to which you will not sink? Excuse me." She and Billy started to walk away.

"Yo, you with the Marilyn Monroe curves!" Flash

called to her. "No need to get so stressed out! This could be your big break!"

Carrie walked away from Billy and back to Flash. "I'm not stressed out," she told him.

"No?" Flash asked.

"No," Carrie repeated. "I'm not stressed out. You're just extremely annoying. You always have been, and my guess is you always will be." She turned and walked back to Billy.

"I am wounded, babe," Flash said gravely, casting his gaze on Sam. "Hmmmm, Big Red, I see you haven't grown any hooters since last we met. But, hey, I can work with that. What say we do the instant-replay lingerie thing? You're a year older, babe, you can sign the release this time."

"Release this," Sam said, bringing her cowboy-boot-clad foot down hard on the toe of Flash's soft white shoe.

"Yeow!" Flash yelped. "Hey, you did that on purpose!"

"Would I do something like that to a nice guy like you?" Sam asked.

"Come on, Leonard, we're outta here," Flash said. He limped away, Leonard trailing behind him.

"That's one part of the island I won't miss," Pres told Sam.

"Oh, don't worry," Sam said lightly. "If we come back next summer, he'll be here, too."

"Next summer's a long time off, little darlin'," Pres drawled. He took her hand.

In the distance she saw Carrie and Billy stop to talk with Molly's parents.

"You think you and Billy will make up?" Sam asked Pres.

"I don't know," he said.

"But how can you stand it?" Sam asked. "If I had a big fight with Emma and Carrie, and the summer was ending, I couldn't stand it."

"Sometimes you can stand more than you think you can," Pres said.

"But Billy is your best friend," Sam said.

Pres nodded thoughtfully. "I guess sometimes even your best friend can turn on you." He wrapped his sinewy arm around her waist. "Come on, let's go dance and have some fun, okay?"

"Okay," Sam agreed. But she couldn't help notice the sadness that filled Pres's eyes. And she didn't know if there was anything in the world that she could do about it.

SEVEN

The sounds of the MORP party still underway back up at the top of the hill filtered down toward Billy and Carrie, where they sat together on a blanket they'd borrowed from the Masons, in a small wooded dell at the edge of the Masons' property. The bright half-moon of late August had risen to a spot in the sky almost directly over them, and the sounds of a whippoorwill in the woods competed with the background noises of the party.

Carrie and Billy had hung out at the party for a couple of hours, dancing, eating, and playing some rather rambunctious party game organized by Molly and Darcy, which involved passing a grapefruit from person to person without using your hands. And then, by mutual silent consent, they'd gone into the house in search of a blanket to borrow so that they could find a place where they could hang out together and talk.

Maybe this will be the moment, Billy said to himself. *Maybe this will be the moment where I can ask her. If I can only get my courage up. I can't believe that I can play music in front of thousands of screaming people, and I'm scared to death of asking Carrie one little question.*

One life-changing little question.

Billy sighed and fiddled nervously with the diamond stud in his ear. *If Carrie says yes, then what?* he wondered. *Should she quit school and tour with me if I form a new band? How can I ask her to do that?*

A few crickets chirped nearby, and a dozen or so fireflies glowed in woods around them, flickering on and off in a dazzling pattern.

"I love the fireflies," Carrie said, the sound of her voice breaking into Billy's thoughts.

"Me, too," Billy agreed.

"And the crickets," Carrie said. "It's almost as if I can hear them saying 'summer's ending, summer's ending.'"

"And it's back to Yale," Billy said, trying to keep his voice light.

"Summer's ending," Carrie whispered again.

"I know," Billy said. He lay flat on his back, looking up at the starry sky.

"Summer's ending," she said one more time. "That's right from *Charlotte's Web*. That's what Charlotte thought the crickets were chirping at the end of the summer. And I think she was right."

Billy reached for Carrie and pulled her down with him. "Don't go getting sad on me, now," he said. "This is a very special moment."

She rested her head on his chest. "Why is that?"

Because I'm trying to get up the nerve to ask you to marry me, he thought to himself. But he didn't say that out loud.

"Oh, you never know," Billy said mysteriously as he stroked Carrie's hair. He chuckled. "And I didn't even know you were a fan of *Charlotte's Web*."

"Oh, yeah," Carrie said. "Big time."

"My mother used to read that book to me when I was like six," Billy reminisced. "Man, I loved that. The soothing sound of her voice, and that great story."

Carrie turned her face toward him. "It just so happens that I can still recite the last paragraph of that book from memory." She cleared her throat ostentatiously. And then she recited the famous last paragraph from E. B. White's book about the odd, dear friendship of a spider and a pig.

"'It is not often that someone comes along who is a true friend and a good writer,'" Carrie recited. "Charlotte was both."

"My mom always used to cry when she read that," Billy said softly. "I never understood why."

"Do you understand now?" Carrie asked.

"I think so," Billy said. He stroked Carrie's cheek. "There's nothing like a real friend, a true friend." A lump formed in Billy's throat as he thought about Pres.

My best friend, he thought. *And a great writer, too. But who knows if we can still be friends after this.*

"It's funny," Carrie mused, "I never used to appreciate how really important best friends are. But now I can't even imagine my life without Emma and Sam, you know?"

Can I imagine my life without Pres? Billy thought to himself. *Can I?*

Carrie tickled Billy's chin with a blade of grass. "You're thinking about Pres, aren't you? I'm sorry the two of you aren't doing so great."

"Me, too," Billy said ruefully. "We haven't had a fight in, like, five years."

"Friends can fight sometimes," Carrie said. "Then they make up."

"Not like this," Billy said firmly. "Pres let me down. He's letting the whole band down."

"Maybe you could talk about it with him and—"

"How about that song he did at the guitar pull?" Billy interrupted, seemingly changing the subject.

"I thought it was really nice," Carrie said. "It made me cry."

"It wasn't just nice," Billy scoffed. "That song was a miracle. That song was fantastic. Do you

94

know how much I'd like to add that song to the end of our act? What rock band do you know would dare do that song? One. Flirting With Danger."

Carrie was silent for a moment, the crickets filling in the quiet moment. "I know it seems like the two of you don't have the same goals anymore, but maybe one of you will change your mind—"

"Well, it won't be me," Billy said. "Pres has given in and given up."

"Maybe what he wants most of all is to be a writer," Carrie said. "That doesn't mean he's giving up."

"He can be a writer and still be in a band," Billy insisted. "Lots of musicians write and tour. Hell, Carrie, we write and tour all the time."

Loud, boisterous cheering erupted from up at the top of the hill.

"Must be more games," Carrie said.

"I don't know what's going to happen with the Flirts," Billy said. "Maybe I'll just form a new band."

"Can you imagine a band without Pres in it?" Carrie asked.

"No," Billy said, sighing. "But I'll learn to deal with it if I have to."

"Let's talk about something else," Carrie suggested, snuggling even closer. She kissed him on the edge of his jawbone.

"Oh, yeah, cool," Billy said, his voice getting a little nervous. He could feel his pulse racing.

This is when I can ask her, he thought to himself. *This is the perfect chance. I've even got my great-grandmother's engagement ring in my pocket. I've been carrying it around for a week now.*

"Are you okay?" Carrie asked him.

"Fine," Billy answered. "I'm fine."

"Your voice didn't just sound fine," Carrie observed. "It sounded . . . weird, or something."

"No, I'm fine. Yep. Fine," Billy said.

All I have to do is ask her, Billy thought. *All I have to do is open my mouth and—*

"Maybe this will make you feel more fine," Carrie said boldly. She leaned over and kissed him on the lips. Billy returned the kiss, sweetly and gently, then more passionately, under the blanket of the starry night sky.

And somehow, Billy never mustered the words he so much wanted to say.

"Mmmmmm," Emma whispered as Kurt kissed her again.

Kurt smiled, and broke away. "I have to get more than my fair share now," he said, "since I've only got three more nights with you."

Emma sighed. "Counting tonight."

"That's right," Kurt agreed. "Counting tonight."

Kurt and Emma had also stayed at the MORP

party for a couple of hours, and then they, too, had slipped away. But rather than find a secluded area on the Masons' property, they'd gotten into Kurt's taxicab, and Kurt had driven them down to the docks on the poorer side of the island, where his dad kept his lobster-fishing boat.

Then, over Emma's mild protests, he'd insisted that Emma climb into an old dinghy, into which he followed her. Then he'd rowed out to his father's boat, which floated on the glassy harbor inlet in the moonlight.

I never would have thought a lobster boat would be romantic, Emma thought to herself. *But this is incredibly romantic. Kurt. And me. And the moon and the stars.*

I wonder what Carrie and Billy are doing right now. And Sam and Pres.

She looked over at Kurt in the moonlight and thought she had never seen a lovelier sight. *What will he say if I tell him that I want to stay here?* she wondered. *Will he be as happy as I think he'll be?*

"Lucky you," Emma said lightly. "You're going to get to enjoy this view all winter long."

Kurt laughed. "I'm not sure *enjoy* is the word, when it's below zero and the wind is howling, and it's snowing so hard the snow comes down sideways. But yeah, I'll be here."

Emma shifted a little bit on the hard bench of the boat and tried to tuck the hem of her short, silk dress under her legs. "I guess I didn't dress exactly right for this outing," she said with a laugh.

"But it's so you," Kurt said, laughing with her.

"Hey, full-time designer wear was the old me," Emma reminded him playfully. "I can wear torn and worn jeans with the best of 'em."

"I know you can," Kurt said, leaning over to kiss her.

"Do you know what you're going to be working on?" Emma asked.

"The boat," Kurt answered.

"I mean, with COPE," Emma said.

Kurt draped his arm around Emma's shoulder. "I met with Jade yesterday," he said referring to Jade Meader, the energetic, older woman who ran COPE. "She was really excited that I'm going to stay here and work with her. She's got a ton of ideas for me."

"How old is she, do you think?" Emma asked.

Kurt shrugged. "In her seventies is my guess. And she has more life in her than most people half her age."

"I know," Emma agreed. "I like her a lot. So what are some of Jade's ideas?"

"Well, for starters, trying to squeeze more money out of the state of Maine to build some new housing," Kurt said as his eyes got a faraway look. "Trying to raise the property tax rates, so that all these summer people who come and use our island in the summer can help the kids who go to school here in the winter. Trying to make sure those developers on Shore Road don't do what they're not supposed to do. And then—"

"And this is just for starters?" Emma interrupted.

"Yeah," Kurt said with a grin. He lifted a lock of Emma's golden-blond hair unconsciously. "It's really important stuff, Em," he added seriously.

"I'd like to help," Emma said softly.

"You help a lot," Kurt said, turning to her. "Jade says that you're the best summer person who's ever worked with COPE. Ever."

Emma smiled a little. "I imagine that's a compliment," she said.

Kurt laughed. "If you know Jade Meader, that's a big compliment. She's not exactly crazy about summer people."

Emma took a moment to get up her nerve. *Okay, just tell him,* she told herself. *Just say it. Out loud.*

"I'd like to help even more," Emma began.

"Well," Kurt said, "next summer—"

"I'm not talking about next summer," she said. "I'm talking about . . . this winter."

He stared at her. "Are you serious?"

"I hope so," she said.

He shook his head with wonder. "You're

something else, Emma. It really means a lot to me that you want to visit the island during your winter break from school and that you'll help with some of the COPE stuff. That would be great."

"I didn't mean on my winter break from school," Emma explained. "What I meant was . . . was that I won't go back to school this year. I'll stay here on the island. The whole winter. Helping with COPE."

Kurt whistled. "Excuse me, but have you lost your mind?"

Emma laughed nervously. "That was not the reaction I was hoping for."

"Well, I'm . . . I'm stunned," Kurt admitted. "I mean, it's hard to picture you—"

"I happen to have a lot to offer COPE," Emma said fiercely. "I'm a hard worker. I think I've proved that."

"Of course you're a hard worker, but—"

"Kurt, don't you see?" Emma asked plaintively. "I've never, ever done a single thing with my life that wasn't about me. Even getting a job as an au pair—that was to prove to my parents that I could be more than just a rich kid. And even the perfume business I started with Carrie and Sam, that was really just a lark. I mean, if it didn't succeed, so what? There was always more money where that came from."

"Emma—"

"No, let me finish," she said. "Working for COPE isn't about money. And it isn't about me. It's about doing something good, something important. And it's something I really, really want to do."

"You're serious," Kurt observed.

"Yes, I'm serious," Emma replied.

"Your mother and father are going to kill you," Kurt said.

"I know. My mother, in any case."

"After she kills me," Kurt amended. "She's going to be certain this is all my idea."

I'm not going to tell him they gave me my money back, Emma thought, *because when they hear this they'll probably just take it away again. And after all, Kurt's always hated my money, anyway.*

"Well, say something," Emma demanded.

"I just want to know that you're sure—"

"I'm sure," Emma said firmly.

"Well, then," Kurt said, "I think it's the most wonderful news I've ever heard."

"Really?" Emma asked, her voice filled with excitement.

"Really. And I want you to know that if you change your mind, it'll be okay—"

"Kurt, I won't," Emma said. "Like you said, I can always go back to college. But for me working with COPE for this year is . . . well, it's like joining the Peace Corps, which you know has always been my dream. Only now I get to do something for someone right here. At home."

"You just called Sunset Island home," Kurt said.

She smiled at him, her eyes filled with tears. "Because it is, Kurt. It is."

EIGHT

"Y'all," Dixie Mason intoned seriously, "last night was the greatest night of my life." In her characteristically soft Mississippi drawl, the word *my* sounded like "mah."

Dixie's accent is so thick it makes Pres sound like he was raised in New York City, thought Sam, who was sitting at the Jacobses' breakfast table with Allie and Becky Jacobs and their friend Dixie, who had spent the night there.

Dan had offered to pay Sam twenty-five dollars if she'd wake up early and prepare breakfast for his daughters and Dixie. So Sam, who was always in need of extra money, had said yes.

Dan couldn't prepare breakfast, Sam thought, *because he was out on a date with Kiki Coors last night. And when I got back from the MORP dance at two-thirty in the morning, he still hadn't arrived back home.*

I guess he was getting really, really close to Kiki

over at her place, Sam thought. *I wonder if they're really serious about each other.*

"Hey, do you think Dad is doing it with Kiki?" Becky asked as she bit into a slice of toast.

"No, I think he stays over at her place and they play Scrabble all night," Allie said sarcastically.

"Wait, are y'all tellin' me that your father is actually, actually—" Dixie couldn't bring herself to say the words.

"Well, yeah," Becky said.

"But . . . he's so old!" Dixie exclaimed.

"What did you guys do last night that has Dixie saying it was the greatest night of her life?" Sam asked, to change the subject.

Even if I'm officially not their au pair anymore, I can't help but try to steer their darling little minds in a healthier direction, she added to herself as she poured herself a cup of coffee.

Dixie's blue eyes glowed with excitement. "It was so fantastic! First Allie gave me a makeover, and then Becky logged me onto America Online on her computer, and then I proceeded to flirt with lots of guys!"

"Dixie leads kind of a sheltered life," Allie reminded Sam.

"Yeah," Becky said. "As soon as she returns to Mississippi, her real life is over and it's back to living like a nun."

"How will I stand it?" Dixie howled.

"You'll manage," Sam said dryly, sipping her coffee.

"But I'm fourteen years old!" Dixie cried. "And my parents treat me like I'm eight!"

"You don't flirt like you're eight," Becky commented.

"It was so much fun!" Dixie cried. "I loved it so much! I wish I could live with y'all. All the time!"

Sam laughed. She liked Dixie Mason, who was Molly Mason's younger cousin. While Dixie was small and blond and bubbly, and had won all sorts of junior beauty pageants in her native Mississippi (before she decided on her own to give it up), Sam knew that Dixie's parents were professors at Mississippi State University in Starkville, and that Dixie was really, really smart. Super-smart, even—her ambition was to be an astronaut.

"Hey, Sam," Dixie called out, "who is the woman in history you most admire, and why? Begin your answer in twenty seconds."

Sam cracked up. Dixie had just posed to her the same question she'd prepped Sam to answer for the Miss Sunset Island pageant earlier in the summer. Dixie had taught Sam the expected answer—Mother Teresa—but when the actual question had been asked, the pageant emcee had asked "who is the woman in history *alive today* you most admire," and Sam couldn't remember if Mother Teresa was alive or dead.

So she'd answered "Carrie Alden."

And she'd come in third.

"I admire Becky and Allie Jacobs," Sam said solemnly.

"Good answer! Good answer!" Becky yelled.

"The reason is," Sam continued, "together, they have enough intelligence to maybe equal one person."

"Hey!" Allie cried.

Becky responded by tossing a piece of dry toast at Sam, who caught it and took a bite.

"You guys know I'm teasing you," Sam said. "You're really smart. And I want you to remember that when school starts in the fall."

"Sam Bridges lecturing us about school?" Allie asked. "But you hate school! You dropped out of school!"

"Well, do as I say and not as I do, okay?" Sam replied.

"Good advice," a voice said from the doorway.

It was Dan Jacobs. He looked surprisingly chipper for someone who had gone to bed just a few hours before.

"Good morning," Sam said. "They're eating."

Dan grinned. "Is there some toast and coffee for me?" He looked at his watch. "I've got an eleven o'clock tee-off at the club scramble."

Sam got up, even though she didn't have to, and poured a cup of coffee for Dan. She handed it to him, after he'd perfunctorily kissed his fourteen-year-old daughters on the tops of their heads. They were deep in conversation with Dixie about the pros and cons of beauty pageants and didn't seem to notice.

"Thanks," Dan said to Sam. "Say, can I talk to you for a minute?"

"Sure," Sam answered.

"In the family room, I mean," Dan said.

Sure, whatever, Sam thought.

Dan had already left the kitchen for the family room, so Sam picked up her coffee cup and followed him. Laughter rang out behind her as Dixie finished telling a story about something that happened to her in a pageant that completely cracked up Allie and Becky.

Dan settled back into his favorite easy chair and invited Sam with a gesture to take a seat on the couch nearby, which she did.

"Summer's ending," he said.

"Guess your golf game will get a little rusty," Sam observed.

"So, Sam," Dan asked, leaning forward confidentially, "what are your plans for the year?"

"Well, everyone keeps asking me that," Sam replied.

"What do you tell them?"

"Let's see," Sam mused. "I was thinking of studying Zen Buddhism in India. Or maybe I'll try the rodeo circuit. I hear a girl can make a mint if she can just learn to rope a steer really well, and—"

"How would you like to work for us?"

"Say what?"

"Work for us. For me," Dan said. "With Becky and Allie. At our house in Boston."

"Oh" was all that popped out of her mouth.

"I guess my offer is something of a surprise," Dan said. "But I've given it a lot of thought. And now I'd like you to think about it, too."

Wow, Sam thought. *I've tried really hard not to think about my future at all, because the idea is just so scary. I have absolutely no idea what I'm going to do with myself.*

I could go back to Kansas, she thought. *I could try to re-enroll in Kansas State University's dance department. But that idea appeals to me as much as eating roadkill.*

Now Dan Jacobs was offering a job.

"What would I do?" Sam asked Dan cautiously.

"Just what you're doing here," Dan replied. "We have a big house in Newton. You'd have your own room, your own phone line, and I'd even get a second car for you to drive."

"Oh," Sam said noncommittally.

"You already said that," Dan pointed out.

"Uh-huh," Sam said. "Um . . . gee, I guess I'm at a loss for words, kind of."

"Sam," Dan said, leaning toward her, his voice

dropped to a whisper. "Becky and Allie need a—someone like you in their lives, Sam. They trust you."

Sam smiled at the irony of it all. Dan Jacobs had almost fired her earlier in the summer for being a bad influence on the twins!

Well, well, how the worm has turned, she thought. *Anyway, I know he's right. The truth of the matter is, I have been good for Becky and Allie. And . . . well, I guess taking care of Becky and Allie has been good for me, too.*

Sam swallowed hard. She knew that Dan Jacobs was right. The twins had never recovered emotionally from their mother leaving them. And Dan, well, Dan had his limitations as a father, to say the least.

"What about Kiki?" Sam asked.

"Well, that's still . . . up in the air," Dan replied. "The relationship is getting more serious, but Kiki has her career to think of."

Yuh, right, Sam thought. *Her big acting career. The one where she never gets any parts.*

"Anyway, Sam," Dan continued, "she isn't you. She doesn't have your rapport with the girls. You are really, really important to them. I hope you know that."

Sam nodded.

"Think about it," Dan went on. "That's all I'm asking."

Sam did think about it. On the one hand, she thought about living in Boston, with a car of her own. Yale and Carrie were just a few hours away by car. Emma wasn't going to be that far away, either. Boston had culture. Boston had modern dance companies. Boston had excitement, and rock concerts, and theater, and fun, and history.

And then there was Kansas. Boring Kansas.

To go back to Kansas would mean I was a failure, Sam thought quickly. *Maybe not for someone else, but it would be that for me.*

It was no contest.

But wait a sec, a voice inside Sam asked. *Are you ready to spend all that time with Becky and Allie?*

"I do it already," Sam said out loud. "What's the difference?"

"Do what?" Dan asked.

"Oh, uh, sorry," Sam stammered. "I'm thinking out loud. I just don't know if working for you would be the right thing to do. . . ."

"I'll double your salary," Dan added.

"I accept," Sam said quickly. She stuck her right hand out.

Dan looked at her hand. "No," he said. "Think about it."

"I've already thought about it," Sam replied.

"Think about it some more," Dan insisted. "Tell

me on Monday morning. Because I don't want the girls to get their hopes up if—"

"If I change my mind," Sam completed Dan's question.

Dan nodded.

"Okay," Sam said. "But there's one thing I want to tell you now."

"What?" Dan asked.

"Thanks," Sam said simply. Then she did something she hadn't done in the two years she'd known him.

She leaned over. And she kissed Dan Jacobs on the cheek to show her gratitude.

At the same time that Dan Jacobs was offering Sam a job with his family at the suburban Boston home, there was an impromptu meeting of Flirting With Danger in the Flirts' living room. But this time, there were no backup singers present. It was just Billy, Pres, Jay, and Jake, sitting on the worn furniture, talking about their future.

The two remaining copies of the songwriting contract from Polimar that Billy hadn't torn up lay on the coffee table, faceup.

Pres looked over at Billy, who wouldn't meet his gaze. *This really stinks,* Pres thought. *I don't see why it has to be Billy's way or no way. I wish I could get through to him.*

Billy finally looked up. "So, you haven't changed your mind, huh?"

"Sure haven't," Pres said. "I say we sign it, we're songwriters, we ease off on the touring for a while."

"We sign it," Billy said, "the band is over. What happens to Jake and Jay?"

Pres shook his head and looked over at Jake and Jay. "I'm truly sorry. But you've got to take your chances in this business. The band's not over. We're just gonna ease back on the touring."

"Meaning you'll drop out of the band," Billy said.

"Meaning I think we can compromise some," Pres countered.

"So, guys," Billy said to Jake and Jay, "our esteemed colleague here wants to be a songwriter. Not a touring artist. Whaddya think?"

Surprisingly, it was mild-mannered Jay, who looked a lot like a young James Taylor, who spoke up first. He looked right at Pres.

"If it were up to me," Jay said, "I'd tie you to your guitar and take you out on the road with us."

"Amen," Billy added.

"But it's not up to me," Jay said. "Pres, it's up to you. You've got to follow your heart."

"Thanks, Jay," Pres said. "My heart says, if Polimar thinks I'm a better writer now than a performer, I want to try that route. What I care the most about is creating the music. That's how I've always felt."

"Jake?" Billy prompted the band's drummer. "You're not gonna let Pres get away with this, are you?"

"Well, you know, Billy," Jake said, "I shouldn't even be here. I'm just a replacement drummer."

"You're a damn good drummer, and Sly would be proud of you," Pres said.

"Thanks," Jake said gruffly. "Well, the way I see it is this. If Pres drops out, Pres drops out," Jake said. "I hate to see him go. But if you go on touring, and you want me as your drummer . . . I'm there. A hundred percent. A thousand percent."

"Me, too," Jay said, taking off his wire-rim glasses and rubbing his eyes wearily. "Billy, I'm with you."

"Thanks," Billy said. "I want you with me. Pres?"

Pres shook his head. "Pardner," he said to Billy, "if it's okay with you, and only if it's okay with you, I'd like to talk to Polimar about maybe joining their staff in Nashville."

Billy and Pres stared at each other.

Come on, Billy, Pres thought. *Don't make us part enemies. We mean too much to each other.*

"It's okay with me," Billy finally said.

Pres's face lit up. "For real?"

Billy gave a short, sharp laugh. "What'd you think, I'd stay mad at you forever?"

"I was kinda worried about it," Pres admitted.

"Well, forget it," Billy said. "I hate like hell to see you leave the band, man. But you do what you gotta do, and you got my blessings all the way. And I'm sorry for what I said about selling out. I didn't mean it that way."

Pres reached over and clasped Billy's hand. "Thanks. That means . . . a lot. So, what are y'all going to do?"

"Find us a new guitar player to play rhythm," Billy said as he reached for a gallon jug of ice water that was on the table. He uncapped it and took a long swallow. "Then go to New Haven, maybe, and start to tour out of there."

"Huh, New Haven," Pres said. "I guess it's more than coincidence that that's where Carrie goes to school."

"You betcha," Billy answered.

"So have you asked—"

"Save it," Billy said, indicating with his eyes that he didn't want Pres to bring up the subject of his possible marriage proposal in front of Jake and Jay. Pres, who'd been touring so long with Billy that he could read his eyes, quickly backed off the subject.

"So, you gonna hold auditions for a new guitar player?" Pres asked.

"We'll start to look after we get to New Haven. That is, if we're all going to New Haven."

Jay nodded.

"I'm in," Jake said. "My money's on the band. Full time."

"We'll miss you," Billy told Pres. "*I'll* miss you."

"You'll know where to find me," Pres said. "Nashville ain't that big a place."

"Correction," Billy said. "You'll know where to find us. And when you're ready, our arms are gonna be wide open for you."

Pres smiled. "I'll send you my best songs."

"You don't," Billy advised him, "you're dead meat."

There was a lot of laughing, and there was a lot of joking, and Pres and Billy even embraced when the meeting was done. But the result was the same. They might still be friends, but Billy and Jake and Jay were going to New Haven to start a new tour, and Pres was going to Nashville to write songs and play sessions.

Flirting With Danger, as they'd all known the band, was history. The name might not change, but the band would never, ever be the same.

NINE

Emma sighed, steeled herself, and gingerly reached for the phone.

"I'm an adult and I am entitled to make my own decisions," she told herself out loud. "I don't have to be afraid of my parents. I mean my mother."

Right. And all she can do is cut off your money again, another voice inside her said. *Then what are you going to do?*

It was later on that same Saturday afternoon. Emma had spent the afternoon putting off, minute after minute, calling her mother and father. She knew she had to inform them about her decision not to return to Goucher College for her sophomore year, but to stay on Sunset Island and work for COPE.

She'd been dreading the moment. Her father might conceivably, possibly, maybe, support her in her decisions, but she had a pretty good idea of how her mother would react.

As Sam said, she'll kill me, Emma thought glumly. *But I've got to do this.* She pursed her lips grimly. *The last time we talked, I told them that I didn't need a ride to school, that instead I was going to take a plane from Portland to Baltimore, and that my clothes and everything else would be shipped. Aren't they going to be in for a surprise.*

Emma sat back heavily on her bed. Then she quickly picked up the phone and dialed the number of her parents' estate on Beacon Hill in Boston.

"Cresswell residence," a female voice answered. "This is Marjorie. May I help you?"

She's one of the new batch of household help my parents have working for them on the weekends, Emma thought, recognizing the voice. *I don't even know her last name. Can you believe that?*

"Marjorie," Emma said, her voice quavering with fear. "It's Emma. Emma Cresswell."

"Yes, Miss Cresswell," Marjorie said formally.

"Please, call me Emma," Emma said awkwardly.

"All right. Emma."

I hate all of this, Emma thought to herself. *Maybe it's because I was away at school so many years, but it doesn't feel like Beacon Hill was ever really my home. Sunset Island is my home from now on.*

"Are my parents there? Could I speak with . . . both of them?"

"I'm afraid not, Emma," Marjorie said. "When

they heard you were going to fly to Goucher on Monday, they left on a short holiday."

"Where did they go?" Emma asked.

"To London," Marjorie reported. "And then to Paris. And then to Majorca off the southern coast of Spain. I think."

"Didn't they leave their itinerary? Didn't they leave a number?"

"Only with their attorney," Marjorie explained. "Mrs. Cresswell insisted that she wanted this trip to be romantic."

"But . . . they didn't even call me to say goodbye or anything," Emma said, hurt.

"I don't know anything about that Miss Cress—I mean, Emma."

"I see," Emma said. And then she realized something. If her parents were out of the country and they hadn't even let her know they were leaving, she couldn't very well be faulted for the fact that they didn't know her plans had changed!

"Please tell them on their return that I called. When are they returning?"

"A good question," Marjorie said. "Ten days, two weeks. Is there an emergency?"

"Oh, no," Emma said lightly. "I just want to . . . to talk to them."

"I shall have them call you at school, then, if—"

"No," Emma said, cutting Marjorie off. "There's no need. I'll call them."

"Very well," Marjorie replied. "It was good speaking with you, Emma. I hope you're enjoying the last days of your summer vacation."

"Oh, I am," Emma said. "Good-bye, Marjorie."

Emma and Marjorie both hung up, and Emma settled her head onto her pillow.

Well, that was a lucky stay of execution, she thought. *But the guillotine is going to drop. I can feel it already. And my neck is the one that's in the stocks.*

We'll see just how stiff a neck I have when I finally do get to talk to them.

"Be strong, Emma," she whispered out loud to herself. "Be strong."

"A letter came for you!" Becky called out as she simultaneously rapped on the door of Sam's room and pushed an envelope through the crack. Then Sam could hear the sound of her shoes banging down the stairs.

"We're going to Ian's for a photo shoot!" Becky called back toward the closed door. "Zit photos. I'll see you later!"

"Later," Sam said laconically, reaching for the envelope.

It was that same afternoon, at about the same time that Emma was on the phone with her parents' housekeeper. Sam had taken advantage of her off-duty status to take a nap, and she had awakened about a half hour before.

And I've been daydreaming about living in Boston since I woke up, Sam thought as she peered down at the letter; actually, an international aerogram.

It was from Israel.

Which meant it could be from only one person. Michael Blady. Her biological father.

When Sam had learned, earlier in the summer, that she was actually adopted, that her parents weren't her biological parents at all, she had completely freaked out. For a long time she felt betrayed, and she couldn't understand how her parents could have lied to her for so many years.

After a while her relationship with them had improved, though it still had a long way to go. And she had also begun a search for her biological parents, which had brought her to her birth mother, Susan Briarly, a book editor in San Francisco. And her biological father, Michael Blady, who was Israeli.

And they were both Jewish.

Which meant Sam was Jewish.

And didn't that blow my mind, Sam thought to herself. *In my tiny town of Junction, Kansas, there aren't any Jews. In fact, the Jacobs family is the first Jewish family I've gotten to know really well.*

Astonishingly enough, Sam had actually now met both her biological mother and her biological father. Michael, whose parents were Holocaust survivors and part of the small Jewish community formerly from Oslo, Norway, had come all the way to Sunset Island. And Sam had stayed in touch with him all through the summer.

And now here was a letter from him, just before the summer was ending.

Sam tore the aerogram open.

But the letter wasn't from Michael.

Oh, there were a few lines at the top from her biological father, but the bulk of it was from Michael's parents, Lillian and Joseph Blady, translated into English by Michael.

Sam read, fascinated:

Dear Samantha,

It has been quite a summer. We have gotten to know you a little bit through your letters, and we have been reunited with our son, Michael. We must say we do not know which has brought us more joy. Both have been a blessing from the Almighty.

We know that your summer is almost over. So we have a proposition for you for your next one! We are not getting any younger, and we long to see our only granddaughter while we can still enjoy the experience! And, Samantha, we know that you are not rich. You have told us that you do not earn very much money as a dancer and an au pair. That is why we wish to invite you to Israel next summer, to visit Michael and us. We will pay the cost of your ticket and your stay.

This is not an extravagance. This is an honor. Please write us and say yes. And we will look forward to next June and count every day until then with happiness.

Your loving grandparents,
Joseph and Lillian Blady

P.S. Michael tells us he will be happy to work as your personal translator with us in the event that you do not learn, by next summer, to speak either Norwegian, Hebrew, Yiddish, or French! We are trying to learn some English. Not so easy!

Sam read the letter once. And then she read it again. And again. And then one more time. And then she marveled at the irony of it all.

She had been the one who had put off thinking about what she was going to do with her life after Sunset Island. While Emma and Carrie were obsessing on it, she was the one who tried to avoid the subject.

And now, her life seemed pretty much in order. She could work for the Jacobs family in the off-season. She could go to Israel next summer. And she didn't have to worry about how she was going to pay for it.

"Wow, Israel," Sam said out loud. "Wait until I tell Pres!"

Pres, she thought to herself. *There's one more thing I can do. I can really work on my relationship with him. No more games.*

So what if I'm afraid that if he gets to know me well enough, he won't love me anymore.

Maybe that's just a chance I have to take.

"You don't think Billy's been acting, well, strange, lately?" Carrie asked Sam and Emma.

"Not at all!" Sam insisted. "He's been acting, well, normal. Really normal."

"You think?" Carrie said.

"I haven't seen anything different," Emma said, agreeing with Sam.

"Maybe it's just when we're alone," Carrie muttered. "But he sometimes gets this really faraway look in his eyes, and then he acts like he wants to tell me something, and then . . . I don't know. It's really strange."

"Oh, it's probably just all this stuff about the Flirts and their deal with Polimar," Sam invented, since she knew that Billy still had not gotten up the nerve to propose to Carrie.

It was later that same afternoon. Emma and Sam had drifted over to Graham Perry's mansion to hang out with Carrie. And besides, they knew that Ian had wheedled Carrie into taking some new publicity photos for Lord Whitehead and the Zit People, as a sort of last-gift-of-summer:

All three of the girls knew that the photo shoot could be the cause of some amusement. So they'd been hanging out for an hour while the Zits prepped themselves for the photos. Emma told her friends all about her decision to stay on Sunset Island, and Sam told all about her job offer from Dan Jacobs, and about the amazing letter that she'd received from her grandparents in Israel. And they'd all talked about the private dates that they had each planned for that evening, with their special guys.

"I guess he's just worried about the band," Carrie said. "But I keep feeling like there's some question he wants to ask."

"Maybe he wants to ask you to marry him!" Emma said.

Sam froze, and then relaxed. *It's okay,* she realized. *Emma was just guessing. She doesn't know anything.*

"Can you imagine?" Carrie breathed.

"Wouldn't that be a romantic way to end the summer?" Emma asked. "What would you say, if he asked you?"

"I might say yes," Carrie replied.

"I knew it!" Sam piped up gleefully.

"And I might say no," Carrie added. "Maybe I'm not ready to get married." She reached under the chaise lounge she was sitting on, took out her camera bag, and started fiddling with the lens on one of her cameras.

"Then there's only one way to find out," Sam declared, pushing her rhinestone-encrusted sunglasses into her hair.

"What's that?" Carrie asked.

"You ask him," Sam said.

"Me?" Carrie exclaimed. "But I'm not sure I want to get married, so how could I—"

"Hey, Carrie!" Ian Templeton called from back by the sliding glass doors to the mansion. "Are you ready? 'Cause we're ready!"

"I'm ready," Carrie said, getting to her feet. "You guys wanna watch the shoot?" she asked her friends.

"I want to stay here and talk about marriage proposals," Sam said.

"Yeah, as long as they're not yours," Emma pointed out.

"Well, I'm allergic to marriage," Sam said with a shudder. "I can't even imagine it. I mean, what's next, *children?*"

Emma and Carrie laughed.

"Come on, you guys. Come keep me company while I take these shots. I need moral support."

Emma and Sam both got up to join her.

"Zits, proceed!" Ian called to the members of the band inside the house.

As Emma, Sam, and Carrie watched, dumbfounded, the Zits trooped out onto the back patio, where they'd previously set up the hulked-out washing machines, dishwashers, microwaves, and other appliances that served as the Zit People equivalent of musical instruments.

I don't know how he did it, Carrie thought, *but he did it. Where did he get those outfits?*

Ian and the Zits looked like aliens from a really low-budget science fiction movie. Or maybe worse.

Each of the band members was clothed in a one-piece, bright-red, rubberized plastic radiation decontamination suit.

Becky and Allie Jacobs had strategically stuffed their decontamination suits so it would appear that they had breasts underneath the rubber. Which they did, of course, but normally breasts don't show under a big, rubber garment.

And the band members had plastic flowerpots on their heads, fastened with chinstraps. Growing out of each of the flowerpots was a single daisy.

"It's a statement," Ian said simply.

"Of what?" Carrie asked him, deadpan, as Ian went about arranging his band.

"Of the eco-terrorism of postmodern industrial society," Becky explained in a withering tone of voice. "Isn't that obvious?"

"And the flowers represent hope," her twin sister chimed in.

"Oh, I get it!" Sam said, hitting herself in the

head. Then she turned and rolled her eyes at Emma, who was standing behind her. Emma did her best to stifle a loud laugh.

"Okay, ready?" Ian asked Carrie.

"Ready!" Carrie acknowledged.

"Go to it, Zits!" Ian commanded, and Lord Whitehead and the Zit People started smashing a single washing machine with iron pipes. Even Ian and Becky and Allie, who usually "sang," had picked up iron pipes and started banging away with gusto.

Carrie started clicking. Ian had wanted "action" shots, and she was determined to give him action shots.

They made an unbelievable racket. It scared a flock of starlings, which had nestled, unnoticed, in the trees on Graham's estate. The starlings whirled overhead, spinning like a dark twister, as they formed a flock to try to fly away and escape the noise.

"Oh, gross!" Sam cried as she felt something yucky land on her arm.

"Oh, no!" Emma wailed as she, too, got zonked by a bird.

Bird poop flew through the air as the frightened flock swarmed above them, and then finally flew away.

Emma, Carrie, and Sam were all hit with major crud. But the Zits came through it unscathed and unmarked.

After all, they were the ones in the decontamination suits.

TEN

"Just two more nights," Pres reflected as he looked west, toward the sunset. It was a glorious Maine evening, and the sun was setting over the mainland.

"Don't say that," Sam ordered, snuggling up next to him on the blanket they'd spread out.

"The truth hurts, huh?" he asked.

"So what if I don't want to face it?" Sam asked. "So what if I can't stand the thought of saying good-bye to everyone—"

"Hey, I understand, darlin'," Pres drawled. "I'm not lookin' forward to facing it, either."

The Sunset Island ferry gave a couple of loud blasts on its horn, warning people on board that they were soon to be docking in Portland harbor, and warning people on the mainland to prepare to board the ferry that would take them to the island out in Casco Bay.

"Ladies and gentlemen and children," came the

announcement over the intercom system. "Next stop and only stop, Portland, Maine. Next ferry for Sunset Island departs in forty-five minutes. The Sunset Island ferry company thanks you for your patronage. And remember, it's easier than swimming!"

Pres and Sam laughed. No matter how many times they'd taken the ferry back and forth to the mainland—and they had done it a lot over the last two summers—the standard ferryboat landing announcement cracked them up.

Actually, it had been Pres who'd come up with the brilliant plan to spend the evening on the ferry. He and Sam had first planned to go for a rambunctious second-to-last evening's date together. The last night was reserved for a final party on the beach with the whole gang. So this would be their very last private date of the summer. They'd decided together to eat at an open-air restaurant on the Portland waterfront, and then go to a new dance club that had opened on Congress Street.

But when Pres arrived at the Jacobses' house to pick Sam up, he'd changed his mind. And when he told Sam his idea, she'd changed her mind. And then she changed her clothes, from one of her Samstyle originals—an antique ivory lace slip with a black velvet vest Sam had created from fabric remnants and then pinned together—to a casual outfit of a cropped white T-shirt, her favorite well-worn jeans, and of course, her red cowboy boots.

It was a glorious night, and it would be a shame to spend any of it inside. So why not just picnic, all night long, on the Portland-Sunset Island ferry? Pres suggested.

"After all, it's the best boatride on the East Coast," Pres had reminded Sam. "And we won't get charged anything extra if we stay on for the return trip."

When the captain saw us spreading out our picnic blanket on the top deck, he did stare, Sam recalled. *And then he laughed. And then he suggested we park ourselves up behind the captain's bridge, where there aren't any people to bother us. And then he sent over a bottle of champagne! Who knows where he got it? I just hope he wasn't planning on drinking it while he was driving the boat!*

"Sunset Island sunset," Sam said with a sigh, staring up at the colorful sky. "One of the last ones for a while." She turned to look at him. "This is too depressing. I mean, I really hate this. Everything feels like the last this and the last that, you know?"

"Yeah," Pres said reflectively as he reached for a strawberry from a Tupperware container. He

131

popped it into Sam's mouth. "Soon I'll be lookin' at some Nashville sunsets."

"What's it like there?" Sam asked.

"It's a great town," Pres said. "Friendly people, great music scene . . . but it's not this."

"No place is this," Sam said, sighing again.

Pres fed her another strawberry. "I hope you'll visit me there real soon."

"You want me to?" Sam asked.

"I just said it, didn't I?"

"I'm fishing for compliments," Sam said primly. "This is where you're supposed to tell me how much I mean to you, and how much you'll miss me, and all that."

Pres ate a strawberry and licked his lips. "An' all that," he finally said.

"What does that mean?" Sam demanded.

Pres shrugged. "I put my feelings better into a song. You gonna take that job with the Jacobses?"

"I think so," Sam said, reaching for another strawberry. "That is, unless you want it."

Pres laughed and pushed some of Sam's wild red hair out of her eyes. "I'll stick to struggling in Nashville, writing songs."

"Oh, good, you can write one about me and tell me how totally crazy you are about me," Sam said lightly.

Pres laughed. "You are somethin' else. Every time I wanted to get really close to you this summer, you pulled away. And now that the summer is ending, you want us to get really close?"

"Maybe I'm growing up or something," Sam said defensively.

"And maybe it's just because the summer is ending," Pres said.

Sam looked away from him. *Come on,* she told herself. *Risk it. Tell him how you feel. No guts, no glory.*

"I've been thinking lately . . . about us," Sam said. "A lot."

"Uh-huh," Pres murmured.

"I know I've been kind of . . . well, kind of flighty sometimes. But I really care about you, Pres."

"I care about you, too," Pres said.

"What I mean is . . . I mean . . ." Sam took a deep breath. "Actually, I . . . I love you."

Pres just stared at her.

"If that isn't good news, it was a joke," Sam said quickly.

Pres laughed and wrapped his arms around her. "Oh, Sam, you are really one of a kind."

"I am?"

"You am," Pres said, still laughing. "It just so happens that I have written a song to the girl that I love."

"And that would be—?" Sam asked meekly.

"That would be for you to hear when you come and visit me in Nashville," Pres said.

"You mean you kind of like . . . um . . . love me?" Sam asked.

"I just said that, didn't I?"

"Well, not exactly," Sam said seriously. "Maybe I'd believe it if I heard the song."

"And maybe you're gonna have to wait until you make the effort to come an' visit me."

"Come on," Sam wheedled. "Don't I deserve to hear it now?" She kissed Pres on the cheek.

"When you come to Nashville," Pres repeated.

"I'll come," Sam said, gently touching Pres's cheek. "I promise."

"It's gonna be so strange," Pres said, shaking his head a little wearily. "No band. No Billy. No gang. No you."

Sam nodded. She could feel herself getting choked up.

"I just can't believe it's ending," Pres said.

"Hey, what's Halloween like in Nashville?" she asked him. "Because I'll be there."

"Warm," Pres said. "Indian summer."

"And you really want me to come?"

"Yeah," he said. "A lot."

"Me, too," Sam replied.

He reached for her and took her into his arms.

"You're the best thing that's ever happened to me," Sam whispered fiercely.

His answer was to hold her even closer. And right then, Sam meant what she had said more than anything else in the entire world.

But now that she knew it, how could she bear to say good-bye?

Miss Rubie, Kurt's adopted aunt, hurried out from behind the counter of her restaurant, Rubie's, to greet Kurt and Emma as they came in the door.

"Emma!" she boomed, her arms outstretched for an embrace. She hugged Emma, then Kurt. "I heard the good news! I understand we're going to have you here all winter!" Rubie's loud, Down East singsong voice got the attention of everyone in the place. Many of the customers turned to look at Kurt and Emma, and smiled.

Emma looked quizzically at Kurt. Yes, she'd spoken to a couple of people besides Kurt about her plan to stay on Sunset Island and work for COPE. But she certainly hadn't told Miss Rubie.

"Sunset Island off-season lesson number one," Kurt intoned. "Sunset Island knows no secrets."

"There's telegraph, telephone, and tell-a-Rubie!" Miss Rubie joked, and all her regular customers laughed at the joke they'd heard a thousand times before.

While Pres and Sam were picnicking on the ferryboat, and Carrie and Billy were sharing a romantic dinner on the back deck at the Sunset Inn, Kurt and Emma had decided to go for one last authentic Maine summer meal at Miss Rubie's.

Not that I won't be in here a lot after tonight, Emma thought happily as she looked around at the familiar, cozy surroundings. *That is, if my parents don't actually murder me for staying.*

Miss Rubie's was not what you would call an upscale place. There were plain Formica tables and somewhat rickety chairs, and plastic mermaids hanging from fishing nets on the walls. Also on the walls were a jumble of photographs of all shapes and sizes: pictures of Sunset Island's working fishing boat crews, with their cod, whiting, and lobster catches.

"So, what's on the menu?" Kurt asked Rubie.

Rubie grinned. "How does fresh boiled Maine lobster, steamers, cole slaw, homemade baked beans, corn on the cob, and a pitcher of iced tea sound?"

Emma smiled. "Delicious."

"Great," Rubie said. "And it's on me."

"Rubie," Kurt said, "you don't have to—"

"Kurt Ackerman," Rubie scolded her adopted nephew, "whose restaurant is this?"

"Yours, ma'am," Kurt answered solemnly, a smile in his voice.

"That's correct," Rubie boomed. "And if Miss

Rubie is offering to take you to dinner in her own restaurant, the proper response is 'Thank you, Rubie.'"

"Thank you, Rubie," Kurt echoed.

Rubie winked at Emma. "You'll have to do a better job training him in manners," she said. "Now, you two take a seat. I'll be right out with dinner for my two favorite COPE workers."

Kurt led Emma by the arm to one of the free booths along the wall.

"She is so terrific," Emma said, reaching for a homemade pickle from the metal dish in the center of the table.

"I know," Kurt agreed. "You'll have a chance to get to know her better during the off-season. Once all the tourists leave, the island changes completely. Rubie has these dinners where the old-timers tell fishing stories that go on forever, but they're great."

"I can't wait," Emma said, smiling at Kurt.

He reached for her hand. "I still can't believe you're staying here."

"Well, I am," Emma said, smiling into his eyes.

"No second thoughts?"

"None," Emma said.

And it's true, she realized. *Ever since I made my decision I've had this wonderful, peaceful feeling inside, like I know it's the right thing for me to do.*

The bells on the front door jingled as the door

opened, and a perfectly aerobicized figure with sexy, curly hair walked in. She was wearing a white bra top under a sheer hot-pink shirt, the world's tiniest cutoff jeans, and hot-pink sandals.

Diana De Witt.

"Well, here comes the appetite-spoiler," Emma said, her eyes on Diana.

"Who'd believe it? Diana De Witt in Miss Rubie's for dinner!" Kurt exclaimed. "I guess she's slumming it."

But Diana didn't go to the counter to sit down or wait for Miss Rubie to seat her. Instead, she walked right over to Emma and Kurt, a huge smile on her face.

"Hi, there!" she said gaily. "May I join you?"

"No," Kurt said. "This dinner is private."

"Oh, really," Diana said, and here her voice changed, to imitate her friend Lorell's Georgia drawl. "I am wounded. Positively wounded."

"We really want to be alone," Emma told her.

Diana leaned against Kurt's side of the table, and Emma winced inside. *I still can't stand seeing her with Kurt,* she thought. *I still can't believe that he actually slept with her.*

"Well, all I can say is, it's truly a shame," Diana said, still leaning toward Kurt. "You'd think that Sunset Island's two year-round COPE do-gooders would have better manners."

"Look, Diana, I don't know who told you that—" Kurt began.

"I guess we'll just have to see if your manners improve in the off-season," Diana said innocently. "You are going to be here in the off-season, right, you two lovers?"

Emma looked at Kurt. Rubie was right. You couldn't keep a secret on Sunset Island. Even Diana knew now that Kurt was leaving the Air Force Academy, and that Emma was going to work on the island for a year, too.

"That's right," Emma said.

"Well," Diana said sweetly, "we'll be seeing a lot of each other, then."

"I thought you were going to Colorado," Emma said, "to college."

"You did?" Diana asked. "What made you think that?"

"Because that's what you told me," Emma said, trying to keep her voice even.

Diana laughed. "Oh, Emma, I was just having a little fun with you. I can't believe you took me seriously."

"Oh, really," Kurt said.

"Really," Diana said, licking her lips sexily. "And since the two of you are such good friends of mine, I thought I'd let you in on my new plans. I'm going to be right here on this cold, windy island, too."

"You're going to stay here?" Emma asked, her voice rising in spite of herself.

"That's right!" Diana said gaily.

"So what are you going to do?" Kurt asked, his voice full of both contempt and disbelief.

"I'm so glad you asked," Diana said, and she plopped herself down in the booth next to Kurt. "Here's my plan. I'm going to work on my writing."

"Your writing," Emma echoed.

"Right," Diana said. "I'm going to try to break into the teen fiction market. Maybe I'll even start a teen series about this island—what do you think? I certainly have the *experience* to do it!"

"That doesn't mean you have the talent," Kurt pointed out.

"Oh, Kurt," Diana said, her voice low and sexy, "you know how talented I am. You didn't forget, did you? Because I haven't."

I'm going to wring her neck, Emma thought. *I'm going to reach over to the other side of this booth and I'm going to—*

"Look, Diana, we can't stop you from staying on the island," Kurt said. "But frankly, neither of us want to have anything to do with you, okay?"

"Oh, Kurt, you never know, you might just change your mind." Diana got up from the booth, and once again leaned toward Kurt. "So, I'll be seeing you around," Diana continued. "Enjoy your dinner. Kurt, I hear it's a long, cold winter here. Great for writing. And snuggling. Bye, Emma."

With that, Diana turned on her heels and walked out the door.

Emma and Kurt just stared after her.

I can't stand not knowing what's going to happen with us, Carrie thought nervously as she looked over at Billy. *Why hasn't Billy said anything to me?*

Carrie and Billy were sitting together at one of the elegant, tableclothed tables on the back deck of the Sunset Inn, overlooking the beach and the ocean. They'd each dressed for the occasion: Billy in jeans, a white linen shirt and a blazer, Carrie in a sheer, floral-print dress that fell gracefully to her ankles.

They'd wanted the dinner to be romantic. And it had been. In fact, they'd stayed so long that they were the last couple left on the deck. A tuxedoed waiter hung by the glass doors leading inside the inn, waiting discreetly for them to leave so that he could clear their table and go home for the night.

And we've managed to talk about everything except what's going to happen with us, Carrie thought as she took another sip of her coffee. *But why?*

"So," Carrie said, trying to sound casual, "it

looks like Emma's going to stay here and work with Kurt, Sam is going to Boston to work for Dan Jacobs, and Pres is going to Nashville. Which leaves you and me . . ."

"You and me," Billy echoed.

"I was kind of hoping you'd finish that sentence for me," Carrie admitted.

"Which leaves you and me going to New Haven," Billy said quietly as he unconsciously fingered the small box in his pocket, which held the family heirloom diamond engagement ring.

Carrie's eyes lit up. "I can't believe that you would do that for me!"

"Car, I'd do almost anything for you," Billy said.

She reached out and took his hand. "You are so terrific," she said.

Ask her! Billy told himself. *Just take out the ring, put it down on the table, and ask her!*

He cleared his throat. "Carrie, I wanted to ask you—"

"But what about Jay and Jake?" Carrie interrupted, her face troubled. "I mean, you guys have to be in the same place if the band is going to—"

"Jay and Jake have agreed to come to New Haven, too," Billy said.

"You're kidding," Carrie uttered.

"I'm completely serious," Billy said. "The three of us are together. The Flirts will go on, minus Pres."

"That's fantastic!" Carrie cried. "And you never know, eventually Pres might change his mind."

Billy shrugged ruefully. "I hope so."

He cleared his throat again and felt his palms getting wet from nerves.

Just ask her!

"Anyway," Billy continued, "you and a band are all I need."

Carrie looked into Billy's eyes. "It means a lot to me that you're coming."

Just ask her!

Billy took a deep breath.

Stop thinking about it, man, and just do it! Now!

He reached into his pocket and took out the small box, the box that held the diamond ring, and he put it on the table.

"Carrie," Billy said, "there's something I want to ask you. . . ."

ELEVEN

ELEVEN

"Carrie Alden, I love you more than anything else in the universe. I will love you forever and ever. Will you marry me?" Billy said inside his head.

Carrie waited. Billy opened his mouth. And then closed it again. And then opened it.

But no matter how hard he tried, or how many times he began to speak, Billy Sampson could not bring himself to say the words.

His mouth just wouldn't form the sentence.

"Carrie Alden, I—" he faltered.

Just say it, Billy told himself. *Say what's in your heart.*

"Yes?" Carrie said, so softly that her words were almost lost in the sounds of the waves lapping at the shoreline.

"This is a ring," Billy finally said, his eyes firmly on the box. "An engagement ring. It's for our engagement."

"Are you—"

"No," Billy fairly whispered. "I'm not. I was going to, but . . ." His voice trailed off again, unable to finish the sentence. He couldn't look her in the eye.

And then he felt her hand on his. "Billy?"

He looked up.

"It's okay."

"It's not okay!" Billy cried. "You must hate me! How could I do this to you, when I love you so much? How could I—"

"Billy," Carrie said, "if I ask you a question, will you answer it?"

He nodded yes.

Carrie smiled at him. "Okay. Here's the question: What makes you so sure that I would say yes?"

Billy's jaw dropped open. "But—"

Carrie laughed. "You don't think it's enough that you're moving to New Haven to be near me?"

Again, Billy couldn't find words to say. "Carrie, I, uh—"

"Billy," Carrie said, "I'm not ready to get married."

"You're not?" Billy asked.

"And neither are you," Carrie surmised. "Or else you would have asked me."

"That's true," Billy said ruefully, looking at Carrie and then again at the box that held the engagement ring.

"When I realized that you were going to . . . well, I thought maybe you were going to . . . ask what you almost asked," Carrie began, "and I had all these different feelings."

"Such as?" Billy prompted her.

"Well, for one thing, I'd be lying if I didn't say that it thrilled me to know that you love me enough to propose," Carrie admitted.

"I do love you enough to—"

"I know that," Carrie said. "And I love you that much, too. But once I got the fairy-tale dust out of my eyes, I realized that I'm not ready to get married. I really want to finish college first, I think. And I'm barely twenty. And well, I guess I'm just not ready."

"But you still want me to come to New Haven?" Billy asked.

"Do I want you?" Carrie looked up at the stars and laughed. "God, it's like a dream come true!"

"But it *is* true," Billy said earnestly. He got up and gently took Carrie's hand, lifting her from her seat. Then, oblivious to the waiter who was still on the deck, he took her into his arms. "I love you so much, Car."

"I know," she said, smiling up at him.

"Someday, when we're both ready, I will be proud to slip that engagement ring on your finger," Billy said.

"And someday," Carrie whispered, her face shining, "someday, I'll be proud to wear it."

Emma and Kurt walked, hand-in-hand, both of them barefoot, along the edge of the calm ocean, toward the dunes at the south end of the beach. They were going to meet Carrie and Billy, and Sam and Pres, for their final farewell to each other, and to the island.

It was, finally, the last evening for the gang on the island. The next day was Labor Day, when everyone was leaving.

Everyone except Kurt and Emma, that is.

Sam is going to Boston with the Jacobs family, Emma thought as her toes splashed through the cold waves halfheartedly splashing at the beach. *And Pres is going to Nashville. And Carrie and Billy will be in New Haven. Which leaves Kurt and me here.*

And I couldn't be happier. Or more nervous. But I am not changing my mind. I'm just not.

The setting sun cast Emma's and Kurt's long shadows out over the ocean. Kurt had a small backpack on, which Emma knew contained something very special. Actually, two very special somethings.

"Whose idea was this time capsule thing, anyway?" Kurt asked Emma.

"Billy's, I think," Emma answered as she stepped

over a small railroad tie that had somehow lodged on the beach near the waterline. "Of course, it might be Carrie's, and she's just giving him the credit."

"Whoever it was, it's a cool one," Kurt said.

"And we'll be here all winter to guard it," Emma said fervently.

"Uh, Emma?"

"Yes?"

"Emma," Kurt said gently, "there's not normally a lot of traffic on this beach in midwinter. I don't think you'll have to guard it too carefully."

Emma smiled. "You can't be too sure," she said. "Especially with Diana De Witt around. I think she would do almost anything to hurt me."

"I'll never understand why she hates you so much," Kurt said.

"Me, either," Emma said. "We were never friends at boarding school. I never did anything to her. And yet she gets such joy out of my pain."

"She's a sick puppy," Kurt said. His eyes slid over to her. "I realize that now."

"There was a time when you didn't," she reminded him.

"I know," Kurt said. "I was a fool."

She smiled at him. "I'm just glad you're not a fool anymore."

He wrapped one arm around her neck, and Emma leaned close to the guy she loved.

I can't believe it's all ending, she thought. *I can't believe all our friends are leaving. But I'm really glad Billy came up with this time capsule idea.*

Billy's concept was for each of them to bring something important and personal to bury in a box by the dunes. Then, next summer, they would all meet at that exact spot on July first and open it together.

And if we're not all there, we don't get to dig it up, Emma recalled. *That's the rule, and we've all agreed. Unless all of us are there, the time capsule will stay buried.*

Maybe forever.

Off in the distance Emma could see a tiny knot of people gathered at the base of one of the dunes.

"There's the gang," Kurt noted.

"I can't believe it's finally over," Emma said softly.

"Actually, it's just beginning," Kurt declared.

"What is?" Emma said.

"The rest of our lives," Kurt answered, holding Emma even closer. "The rest of our lives together, I hope."

"I hope so, too," Emma said softly. "So much."

Kurt stopped and turned to Emma. The setting sun illuminated her blue eyes and shiny blond hair.

"Do you mean that?" he asked fervently.

"To spend the rest of our lives together?" Emma asked. "Why do you think I would stay here on the island with you this winter if I didn't want—"

"I thought you were doing it for COPE," Kurt said honestly.

"I am doing it for COPE," Emma said. "But what good is working for something you believe in if the person you believe in is far away?"

"Really?" Kurt asked.

"Really."

"Because Emma, I was thinking," Kurt murmured. "I want to spend the rest of my life with you, too."

"But, Kurt, the last—"

"The last time I was young and dumb," Kurt said. "And I'm still young and dumb. But I know what I want. And it's you."

"I just don't want to rush—"

"I'm proposing," Kurt said, taking Emma by both hands. "Not that we get married. Or engaged, even. How about engaged to be engaged."

"Engaged to be engaged," Emma repeated.

"Will you—"

"Yes," Emma said. "Yes, yes, yes."

And then Kurt took Emma into his arms and kissed her, with a kiss that seemed as if it would last a lifetime.

A lifetime together.

*   *   *

The six friends stood in a circle on the sand, all around a deep pit dug at the base of one of the dunes.

Next to the pit was a huge pile of sand, with a shovel stuck in it. And next to the shovel was a big metal box.

The time capsule.

The time capsule that would be sealed, and buried, and not opened again unless each and every one of the six came back to the same spot, the next summer, at sunset on July first.

Kurt, who was going to spend the winter on Sunset Island.

Emma, who'd be there with him.

Sam, who was going to work in Boston, and who was hoping to go to Israel at some point the next summer.

Pres, who was headed for Nashville.

Carrie, going back to Yale and New Haven.

Billy, who was going to build a new Flirting With Danger, with his base in New Haven, too.

They'd all arrived at the dune an hour before. They all knew that Billy and Carrie were not getting engaged yet. And they all knew that Emma and Kurt were engaged to be engaged.

And now they stood, in a big circle, all holding hands, ready for their final time together.

"Who's gonna be first?" Billy asked.

"I will," Emma said, being uncharacteristically bold. She dropped hands with Kurt to her left and Pres to her right, and reached into Kurt's backpack.

She took out a beautiful covered diary.

"My aunt Liz gave me this diary when I came to the island last summer," Emma said, choking back her tears. "This diary means everything to me. And so much of it belongs to all of you, especially to Carrie and Sam. So it will wait here, until next summer, for me to write in it again."

Emma walked over to the open metal container and lovingly placed her diary in the bottom, and then returned to her place in the circle.

Billy was next. He put in the original lyric sheet of a song he'd written about Sunset Island and Carrie, a song called "Dreams of Home."

Then came Kurt. He took a sealed envelope with some pebbles in it out of his backpack, walked over to the capsule, shook the pebbles so they rattled around a bit, and then dropped the envelope inside.

"These pebbles are from the Hewitts' backyard," Kurt explained as his friends looked at him quizzically. "Just ask Emma, she'll explain."

Emma felt as if she was laughing and crying at the same time. "I can't explain," she managed to choke out. "But believe me, those pebbles are very special."

"I reckon I'm next," Pres drawled. He walked over to the time capsule and stood next to it.

"Hey, big guy," Sam called out, "you gotta put something in it, and you won't fit!"

Everyone laughed, but also waited expectantly to see what Pres was going to do.

He reached in his pocket.

He took out the keys to his motorcycle.

He dropped the keys in the time capsule.

"I won't be wanting my bike in Nashville," he explained, "'cause I know the folks there drive like idiots. So I figure I'd better leave it here. But if we all don't come back next summer, I don't figure to be doing much riding."

"Why not?" Carrie asked.

"Because I only ride that bike when I'm happy," Pres said. "Without all of you back here with me, well, I don't figure I'd be in for very much of that." He rejoined the circle, and Sam leaned over and kissed his cheek.

The evening light was fading now, and in the sky above them, the brightest stars were beginning to glimmer.

It can't be over, Sam thought. *It just can't be.*

"Who's next?" Kurt asked.

"I guess I am," Carrie said. She walked over to the time capsule and looked inside it. Then she reached down for a package that was next to it and picked it up.

"Don't tell me," Sam said. "It's a cassette tape of the Zits' greatest hits."

Everyone laughed, grateful for the comic relief.

"That would have been a good idea," Carrie said. "But actually, it's a cassette recording of a letter I wrote and then read out loud into my tape recorder, a letter to all of you."

"Don't we get to hear it?" Billy asked.

"Not until next summer," Carrie said. "I hope."

All eyes turned to Sam.

"I don't want to do this," she said fiercely.

"Why not?" Kurt asked.

"I know why," Emma said softly. "Because you don't want this to have to be the end. . . ."

"So?" Sam asked. "So I'm a big weenie, I can't help it—"

"It's okay, Sam," Pres said, squeezing her hand. "We're all right here with you."

Sam waited a moment, then she shook her head yes. "Anyone have a flashlight?" she asked.

"What for?" Billy asked her.

"Never mind what for, just give me one," Sam instructed.

Fortunately, Billy did bring a flashlight with him, thinking that the evening might stretch into the night. He tossed it to Sam, who took something out of her shoulder bag.

She shined the light on a photograph.

"Flash Hathaway, eat your heart out!" she yelled

at the top of her lungs, showing the illuminated photo to her friends as she yelled.

It was one of the sexy lingerie photos that Flash had taken of Sam the first summer on the island. In it, Sam was in a transparent white baby-doll, her long red hair flowing down over the front of it.

"This photo caused me a lot of grief," Sam declared, "but it belongs in here."

She dropped it into the time capsule, where it fluttered to the bottom.

"Maybe that little number should stay buried, even when we dig this puppy up next summer," Pres suggested.

"Tell you what," Sam said. "Next summer when we all meet here to dig this up, we will have the joy of torching that photo together, okay?"

"It's a deal," Pres said, and everyone agreed.

It grew quiet. They stood in a circle, their hands joined once more.

"Well, I really hate this a lot," Carrie finally said.

"It's not forever," Emma said. "It can't be."

"It won't be," Billy said firmly. "Hey, I've got an idea! How about if we all show up at the Jacobses' house outside of Boston one weekend this winter? You'll be needing a break from the twins, won't you, Sam?"

"Actually, I won't be with the twins," Sam admitted.

"What do you mean?" Carrie asked her.

"Well, I've been thinking," Sam said. "I can't go to Israel next summer and be here with all of you at the same time. So . . . there's been a change of plans."

"Did you plan to let us in on them?" Pres asked dryly.

"Sure," Sam said nervously. "What I'm going to do is . . . I'm going to Israel. Tomorrow. And I'm going to stay there until May. And work on a kibbutz. A kibbutz is—"

"A communal farm, basically," Carrie filled in. "I know what a kibbutz is, but . . . I'm stunned."

"We're all stunned," Emma said. "When did you plan all this?"

"Um . . . recently," Sam admitted. "I called Michael, and he was all for it. And I still have my passport from when I was going to go to Japan and dance, and I even got up the nerve to tell my parents—in Kansas—and they said it was up to me, and—"

"Sam," Carrie began, "do you realize that working on a kibbutz is—"

"Really hard work," Sam finished for her. "I can work hard."

"You?" Kurt asked skeptically.

"You think working with Becky and Allie Jacobs is *easy?*"

"It's not the same," Kurt pointed out. "You sure you can handle it?"

"No," Sam admitted. "I'm scared to death. But . . . I'm going to try my best."

"But Sam," Kurt said, "I still don't get it. Why would you go work on a kibbutz instead of staying with your Israeli relatives?"

Sam scratched a mosquito bite on her arm and shrugged. "Well, it's kind of like this. I don't really know them. I mean, I want to get to know them, but . . . I want to have some independence too, you know?"

"And another thing," Kurt continued. "You don't know any Hebrew, do you?"

"No," Sam said. "But I can learn, can't I? They have this really accelerated program on the kibbutz where they teach you Hebrew. I can learn. I'm not stupid."

"I never said you were stupid," Kurt said, "but—"

"Hey, quit doubting Sam!" Carrie said mildly.

"Yeah, quit doubting me," Sam echoed. "I'm turning over this new leaf and everything."

Kurt grinned. "Okay. You've won me over, Sam. I'm with you all the way."

Pres hugged her hard. "Me, too, darlin'. I'm proud of you."

"You are?" she asked him.

He nodded. "I know you can do it, too."

"You're not mad that I won't be able to come see you in Nashville?"

"You gotta do what you gotta do," Pres said. "And I know this means a lot to you."

"Will you write to me?" Sam asked, her eyes filling with tears.

"You won't be able to stop me," Pres said, hugging her again. "You're one of a kind, girl."

"Yeah, to know me is to love me," Sam quipped, wiping a tear from her eye.

"So, are we ready to fill this in now?" Billy asked, reaching for the shovel.

Sam took it from him. "Allow me. I'm the one who's heading for some serious manual labor."

"Not so fast," Billy said. "One more thing."

He stepped out of the circle and reached into a bag by his side.

"Look at this," he commanded, taking a photo out of the bag. He passed the photo to Carrie, who looked at it for a long time, and then gave it to Kurt. Who gave it to Emma. Who gave it to Pres. Who gave it to Sam. Who, after looking at it for an eternity, gave it back to Pres.

It was a photo of the original Flirts, with Emma and Sam as backup singers. Carrie was sitting with the band, and Diana De Witt was nowhere to be found.

And Sly Smith, the original Flirts drummer, was behind his drum kit.

"It's only right," Billy said. He went over to the capsule and lovingly placed the photograph in the bottom. Then he closed the capsule, sealed the top with waterproof tape, and lowered it into the hole in the sand. With a sigh he took the shovel and started filling it in.

One by one, each of the friends took a turn at the shovel until the capsule was buried beneath the sands of Sunset Island's beach.

And then Billy started to sing.

> I've traveled far from where I started
> Didn't know just where I'd end.
> I met a lot of folks along the way
> Some that I'd call friends.

> But I just kept on keeping on
> Restless as a rolling stone.
> Until the day I found this island.
> And I knew that I was home.

They all knew the song well. Billy and Pres had written it together, and it was a regular part of the Flirts' act. And they all started to sing the chorus together, at first slowly and hesitantly, then stronger.

> Home is where the heart is
> Home is where you're loved
> Home is where you make your dreams come
> true
> Dreams of home, dreams of you.

By unspoken agreement, they let Billy take the next two verses by himself.

> Now I have loved and lost before
> Didn't know I'd hurt so bad.
> And I have had some fine, sweet times.
> I've been happy, I've been sad.

> But something made me wander
> Something made me roam
> Until the day I found this island
> And I knew that I was home.

And then they joined in for the chorus once again. In the act on stage they usually repeated it twice. But tonight they repeated it three times, as if none of them ever wanted to let the summer end.

> Home is where the heart is
> Home is where you're loved
> Home is where you make your dreams come
> true
> Dreams of home, dreams of you.

And finally the song reached its last words. The circle had reformed on the beach as the friends stood hand-in-hand around the buried capsule.

There was no more singing. There was just the sound of the gentle waves on the sand and a few brave crickets in the dunes.

"Summer's ending," they chirped. "Summer's ending."

The crickets, Carrie thought as tears slid down her face, *are never, ever wrong.*

TWELVE

"I can't believe you only have one bag and you're going to Israel for who knows how long," Emma marveled.

Sam shrugged. "Michael says I won't need a lot of clothes on the kibbutz. Besides, I have to buy clothes there, don't I?"

"Of course you do," Carrie said. "I got worried there, for a moment."

The three girls stood together at Gate 14 at the Portland Airport. Sam's plane for Boston, where she would be making a connecting flight to Israel, was boarding in five minutes.

"You guys will write to me, won't you?" Sam asked.

"We've already told you a hundred times that we would," Carrie said gently.

"Yeah, well, so what if I need reassurance," Sam said. She flipped some of her wild red hair out of her eyes. "I'm glad it's just the three of us. I would have been such a wreck if Pres was here."

"Was it hard to say good-bye to him this morning?" Emma asked.

"Real," Sam said. She gulped hard. "The only thing harder is saying good-bye to the two of you."

"Don't start crying again," Emma warned. "Because if you start, then I'll start, and then Carrie will start, and then we'll never stop."

"What if it turns out this was the stupidest thing I ever did in my life?" Sam asked. "What if I hate it there? What if my family hates me? What if everyone on the kibbutz hates me? What if—"

"Time out," Carrie said. "Take a breath, at least."

"I'm a wee bit nervous," Sam said meekly. "You guys are really lucky. You're both gonna be with your boyfriends. But Pres and I will be so far apart. You think he'll forget all about me?"

"No one could forget all about you," Emma told her.

"Some fine little hussy in Nashville could steal his heart," Sam said. She shook her head ruefully. "I have this terrible feeling in my stomach, like I made the stupidest decision in my life."

"You don't have to get on the plane," Emma said. "It's not too late."

"No, I want to," Sam said. "But I'm scared I'll lose Pres. Just when I finally admitted to him how I feel about him. And then like the same idiot I've always been, I run away." She buried her head in her hands. "Someone just shoot me and put me out of my misery!"

"Flight four-thirty-seven for Boston will now begin boarding at Gate Fourteen," a smooth female voice said over the PA system. "All first-class passengers, or those needing a little extra time, may board at this time."

Sam raised her face from her hands. Her skin was white underneath her tan. "What am I doing?"

"Sam, really, if you don't want to go—" Emma began.

"I do," Sam said. "I really do. I just . . . I wish I could clone myself! And one of me could be somewhere close enough to Pres to see him every few weeks."

"I just have a feeling everything is going to work out," Carrie said firmly.

"You do?" Sam asked.

"I do, too," Emma said.

Sam's eyes searched theirs. "I believe you guys. Which is crazy, I know, but for some crazy reason, I believe you."

"Passengers on flight four-thirty-seven to Boston who are sitting in the rear of the plane, rows thirty through forty-two, may now board the plane at Gate Fourteen," the voice said through the PA.

Sam looked at the ticket in her hand. "I'm in row thirty-eight," she said. "I guess that's me."

"We'll miss you, Sam," Carrie said softly.

"So much," Emma added.

Tears slid down Sam's cheeks. "This is really it? The end of the summer? The end of us?"

"Not the end of us," Emma said as tears slid down her own cheeks.

"That will never happen," Carrie added fervently. "One for all and all for one, right?"

"Forever," Emma nodded.

"Forever," Sam said.

And then the three girls put their arms around one another, and they cried so hard that each felt as if there couldn't be that many tears.

"I love you guys," Sam said hoarsely, pulling away from them. "You're the two best friends I ever had in my life."

"We'll see you here next summer," Carrie said. "July first. Promise!"

"I promise!" Sam said.

"Me, too," Carrie said.

"Me, too," Emma added. "And we'll always be together, in our hearts."

Sam lifted her carry-on bag, and after one last look at Emma's and Carrie's tear-stained faces, she turned around and headed for the plane.

I won't look back, she told herself. *If I look back, I'll never get on that plane.*

Sam stowed her carry-on bag in an overhead bin, then found her window seat near the back of the plane. She was so busy crying that she was barely aware when the plane began to taxi down the runway, and finally took off into the clear sky, carrying her away from the island and the people she loved.

Sam wiped at her tear-filled eyes and looked out the window so that she could catch a last look at the island below her. *This is what it feels like when your heart is breaking,* she thought as she watched the island getting smaller and smaller.

And then she felt a tap on her shoulder.

"Is this seat taken, darlin'?"

Sam turned around. And standing there, with a big grin on his handsome face, was Pres.

She blinked twice. "Am I seeing things?" she whispered.

He slid into the empty seat next to her. "I got assigned a seat up near the front," he said. "I guess we kinda missed each other getting on the plane."

"But what . . . how . . . ?" Sam stammered.

"Well, it's like this," Pres said. "Once, a long time ago, you told me you were goin' to go to Israel one day, to get to know your dad and to meet your grandparents. And if you think back, you'll remember that I told you I'd come with you. Well, I guess you could say I'm a man of my word."

Sam was crying even harder now, but they were tears of happiness. "I can't believe you surprised me like this. And I can't believe you meant it when you said you'd come with me. I just, I can't—"

"I love you, Sam Bridges," Pres said. "And I'm here for you."

Then Sam was in his arms, and they were both laughing and crying, and together they pressed their faces to the window of the airplane.

And maybe it was only their imagination, but it seemed to them they could still see a last glimpse of their beloved Sunset Island, the place where dreams came true, as they headed toward the future.

SUNSET ISLAND MAILBOX

Hey Readers!

You never thought that the endless summer was going to come to an end, did you? But now it has, and Emma, Sam, and Carrie are all off on their separate adventures. My publisher tells me that if Sunset Forever does well, they may publish even more books, about what happens next summer on the island. So Sunset Forever is a book that you and your buds just have to have in your collections!

So . . . what did you think about how the summer ended? Write to me and let me know.

A little news from Tennessee: Jeff and I are doing great and working on all kinds of writing projects, from books to plays to television. We've traveled a lot this past year and met many, many of you. And remember—if you come to Nashville, Jeff and I will take you out to lunch. Just give us some advance notice. By the way, your parental units will have to sit at a table in a different section of the restaurant.

Let's go to the mailbox and see some of what's come in lately. Your Canadian Sunset sister Marta George, in Petrolia, Ontario, sent me a friendship bracelet, and says she's wearing the identical bracelet! Victoria Caffee in Gardendale, Alabama, wants to know if there'll be a sequel to Sunset Wedding. Victoria, after reading this book, what do you think now? Jennifer Russo from Warren, Michigan, sent a great photo, and told me she found a tiny Sunset Island on a map of Maine. Too cool! And Sunset sister Rebecca Tigerman from Seattle, Washington, says her summer project this summer is to read each and every one of my books. Go for it, Rebecca!

We got some bad news this week, and I really want to share it with you. A great teen girl we know was killed in an auto accident. She was in the back seat of a car, and did not have her seat belt fastened. Please, please, please . . . always click that seat belt closed.

So, that's it for this book. I hope to see you in the backs of many, many more books to come. Keep those cards and letters coming, and photos. Every letter gets a personal response (though second letters need to come with a self-addressed, stamped envelope: the volume is getting overwhelming!). Find me online at authorchik@aol.com and I'll hook you up with some keypal Sunset Sisters. Have a great summer. And I'll always see you on the island!

See you on the island!
Best-
Cherie Bennett

Cherie Bennett
c/o General Licensing Company
24 West 25th Street
New York, New York 10010.

Dear Cherie,

I just read another book of yours. It was really good. Pretty soon I am going to the bookstore to buy book #14, Sunset Embrace. *The characters in your books are so realistic. I'm so glad you wrote the* Sunset Island *series, and I hope you will continue your series as Sam, Carrie, and Emma graduate from college, get married, and have children.*

> *Sincerely,*
> *Brittany Michelson*
> *Prescott, Arizona*

Dear Brittany,

What a great letter. You've got a lot of terrific reading ahead of you. But don't be too sure about Emma, Sam, and Carrie graduating from college, getting married, and having children. As you can see in this book, anything can happen . . . and usually does!

> Best,
> Cherie

Dear Cherie,

Wuz up? Our names are Sarah and Rachel and we're in the eighth grade. We love your books. Since you always ask the readers' opinions, we have an idea. We think you should write books from the guys' point of view. We would also like for you to tell us more about the play Anne Frank & Me. *In school we have been reading* The Diary of Anne Frank, *and we would love to see your play, it sounds great.*

    P.S. What do you think of the Indians (baseball team)?

> *Love always and 4-ever,*
> *Sarah Laub and Rachael Zanotti*
> *Parma Heights, Ohio*

Dear Sarah and Rachael,

You should be happy with this book, because there's a lot of times when I got inside the heads of the guys. <u>Anne Frank & Me</u> is now published by one of the major play publishers, Dramatic Publishing Company—you shouldn't just see it, you should talk to your school drama coach about putting it on at your school! As for the Indians, I don't live in New York City anymore, but I sure have a soft spot for the New York Mets!

Best,
Cherie

Dear Cherie,

Do you remember me, Tara Drollinger? I decided to write you 'cause while in a bookstore I saw some new books by you. You should write something in your books about someone dying and how they handled it. Recently a very close friend of mine was in a car accident and died. Now, I buckle and rebuckle my seat belt, and every time I think of something he and I did together, I cry.

Love and luck from your #1 fan,
Tara Drollinger
Weaver, Iowa

Dear Tara,

I am so sorry to hear about your friend. That is a true tragedy. If you read my letter to readers, we have been shocked by something similar that happened here. Many readers have written to me about <u>Sunset Secrets</u> and <u>Sunset Spirit</u>, and how they learned important lessons from those books. I wish you all the best. Please take care of yourself. I want you to be around for about the next hundred years!

Best,
Cherie

If you enjoyed the Sunset Island™ books, don't miss the new series by Cherie Bennett and Jeff Gottesfeld. . . .

Here is an excerpt from *Trash*, the first book in the series, available from Berkley Books . . .

"My father was a mass murderer."

Chelsea Jennings took a shaky breath and leaned forward into the microphone.

"Did I forget to mention that? Maybe you've heard of him—Charles Kettering? That's right—the guy who went into the Burger Barn Restaurant in Johnson City, Tennessee, oh, about seventeen years ago, and shot every single person inside on one sunny Monday afternoon.

"Then he drove home—I mean, no one in the restaurant was left standing to stop him—and I guess his plan was to murder Mom, too—even though she did have his favorite lunch all ready for him on the dining room table. He probably planned to kill me, too—but hey, I was only ten months old, so I don't really know.

"Anyway, Mom ended up killing Dad instead—lucky for me, huh? And then, of course, Mom and me moved to Nashville and changed our name, and then after that I really had a very normal life.

"Oh, and don't worry. I'm not much like him. I don't even have a bad temper—ha ha.

"What else? Let's see. I'm valedictorian of my senior class. I'm a very hard worker. Oh, and I'm very interested in a future career in television. Which is why it means so much to me that you have hired me as a summer intern on your television show, *Trash*."

Chelsea put down her "microphone"—actually, the hairbrush she had been *pretending* was a microphone—and stared at her reflection in the mirror over her dresser: shoulder-length golden-blond hair, large green eyes—all in all, a pretty, all-American-looking face gazing back at her. At the moment, she was dressed in jeans, hiking boots, a man's white T-shirt with a beige suede vest over it, and a gold-and-black Vanderbilt University baseball cap perched backwards on her head.

Normal, she told herself. *I look totally normal. Like any other eighteen-year-old girl going off to New York City for her very first summer job as a TV intern.*

"It's a good thing being the only child of a psychokiller doesn't show on your face," she told her reflection. "Of course, if you'd told them the truth, you'd probably be a guest on *Trash* instead of an intern working for it."

No one knew the horrifying truth about her father except Chelsea and her mother, and they never, ever talked about it. In fact, they both pretended that it had never really happened.

And most of the time, it doesn't seem as if it ever really did happen, Chelsea thought. *I can go days, weeks, sometimes even months, just living my life, hanging out with my friends, just normal me with my normal life.*

Except that my real name is Chelsea Kettering.

And, up in the attic, hidden away, are the yellowed newspaper articles, the front-page headlines, about wealthy Johnson City attorney Charles Kettering, who just went bonkers one day and shot twenty-three people in a fast-food restaurant, and about his wife, Arlene, who stabbed her husband with a kitchen knife so he couldn't get to their innocent baby daughter.

And the front-page photos of me, the poor, innocent baby, wrapped in a white blanket with a duck on it, being carried out of the Ketterings' palatial home by some social worker.

Chelsea shook off her musings and picked up the glossy folder that lay on her dresser. The word *Trash* was written on it in huge, raised neon letters. The folder had arrived in the mail a month earlier, and still Chelsea found it all somewhat hard to believe.

Chelsea's dream, ever since she could remember, was to one day become a producer of some important television news show such as *Sixty Minutes*. She had no desire to be in front of the camera—in fact, the very thought made her cringe. Rather, she wanted to be the one who made it all happen, who pulled the strings, uncovered corruption, spoke for the powerless, and hopefully made the world a better place.

Corny, but true, Chelsea thought. *And TV— really good TV—can do all that.*

However, Chelsea knew that thousands—even tens of thousands—of high school graduates wanted careers in TV, too. And she knew that many of them began by getting internships in the industry the same summer they graduated from high school.

An internship would be the all-important foot in the door, crucial if one had any hope at all of succeeding.

That's when Chelsea had come up with her game plan: she would spend three months of the fall of her senior year applying for every single TV internship available to graduating high school seniors in the entire country. And then she'd be able to pick and choose among all the ones that offered her an internship.

So she spent all her money from her after-school job at The Gap on postage and printing. She sent packets about herself everywhere, from prestigious places like *Sixty Minutes* (her dream) to the lowest-rated local TV station in Nashville. When she had exhausted all possibilities, her records showed she had applied for three hundred and forty-eight internships.

She was turned down by three hundred and forty-seven.

It was the biggest ego-bruiser of her life to date.

Oh, she'd been a finalist for an internship at a local station in Nashville, but she hadn't even gotten that.

It turned out that being the best and the brightest at her high school simply put her up against the best and the brightest from thousands of different high schools across America. In other words, she was utterly ordinary. Didn't stand out.

Didn't get picked.

Except by *Trash*.

Trash, of all places.

Trash was the number one–rated talk show on TV. Geared to a Gen-X and teen audience, it was the most audacious show that had ever been on the airwaves. Frankly, Chelsea thought it was a pretty awful show, but she applied for the internship simply because she was applying for every single TV internship that existed.

Never in a million years did I think I had a shot, Chelsea thought. *And I still have absolutely no idea why they picked* me.

After all, on paper I look so normal, and Trash *is anything but! So what if I graduated number one in my class, and so what if I was editor of the Hume-Fogg Honors High School newspaper*, The Foghorn? *Those credentials must be a big yawn, or else some other TV station or some other TV show would have offered me an internship.*

But no one did.

She figured maybe it was the first-person essay she had written for her *Trash* application that had done the trick.

The directions had instructed her to "be wild and fearless, just like *Trash*."

So Chelsea had written her essay as if she were a teen runaway and drug addict, a prostitute on the streets doing whatever she had to do for a fix.

And it wasn't until the end of the essay that she had admitted that none of it was true, but she added that she believed a real journalist should be willing to go anywhere and do anything to get a true story.

Yeah, like I'd really go live on the street and sleep with strange men and become a drug addict for a story, Chelsea thought. *I am the most clean-living, virginal, normal (or so they* think), *boring eighteen-year-old left in Nashville, Tennessee. And why* Trash *picked me when every place else in the entire country turned me down, I cannot imagine.*

But they did. And it's a famous show. And I'll get

to live in New York. And I'll actually be working in TV. Hey, it's a foot in the door. It's a start. Thousands of kids didn't get picked at all.

Chelsea ran her fingers over the raised letters on the cover of her folder from *Trash*, then opened it and read, yet again, the tantalizing letter that was enclosed.

Dear Chelsea,

Congratulations!

Out of over ten thousand applicants, you have been selected as one of the six summer interns for *Trash*, the most controversial and hippest teen TV talk show in America today.

Rolling Stone calls us hipper than MTV's *The Real World*. The *New York Times* says we make Ricki Lake's show look like *Mister Rogers' Neighborhood*, and our ratings prove that we are a national phenomenon, expressing the daring, cutting-edge of American youth today.

This summer, you will be a part of it.

Enclosed is all the information you will need regarding your housing in New York, job description, etc.

Trash. Excess/Access/Success.

Welcome aboard.

Barry Bassinger, Senior Producer.

Chelsea flipped to the next page, which gave directions to the apartment on the Upper West Side of Manhattan that she would be sharing with the two other female *Trash* interns, only four blocks from the studios where *Trash* was aired daily in front of a live studio audience.

My own apartment, Chelsea rhapsodized. *And no mom there to have an anxiety attack if I'm five minutes late, or if I actually have a date with a guy she doesn't know, or—*

"Chelsea, honey?"

She quickly closed the folder and turned around. Her mother was standing in the doorway of her room, her face even more anxious-looking than usual.

"Hi, Mom," Chelsea said, giving her mother a reassuring smile.

Her mother's eyes swept across Chelsea's packed suitcase and the small carry-on case with the rolled-up copy of *People* magazine sticking out. "So . . . all ready," her mother said, a slightly desperate edge to her voice.

"Please don't be upset, Mom—"

"I'm not," her mother said as she nervously patted her perfectly coiffed hair into place, which she always did when she was upset.

Chelsea tried to see her mother as a stranger might—the perfectly pressed navy pants and matching blazer, the understated strand of real pearls around her neck, the tasteful makeup on her attractive, unlined face.

Her mother always looked perfect. She taught music at an exclusive, private girls' school; she was on the board of a number of charities; and she sang in the church choir. In fact, everything on the outside was always perfect—clothes, hair, home, daughter.

To hide what's going on inside, Chelsea thought. *To hide our horrible secret.*

"So, I guess we'd better leave for the airport," Chelsea said, picking up her purse and slinging the strap over her shoulder.

"New York is so far away . . ." her mother began.

"It's going to be fine, Mom," Chelsea said. She had been saying the exact same thing for a month, ever since she had received the letter in the mail telling her that she had actually been picked for the *Trash* summer intern program.

"Well, I'm going to worry about you in that city all by yourself," her mother insisted, her brow furrowed.

"I'll be fine," Chelsea said again. She picked up her suitcase and headed for the stairs.

"I still don't understand why you couldn't have accepted an internship from a nice show," her mother said, trailing behind her.

"Mom, this is an incredible opportunity," Chelsea

maintained. She hadn't admitted to her mother that every other internship in the entire country had turned her down.

She had been too embarrassed.

"It's just that I've heard that *Trash* is just so . . . so . . . unsavory," her mother said, fiddling with her pearls. "I have friends who watch it. Evidently they have on drug addicts! And gang members. And homosexuals—"

"We have all that right here in Nashville, Mom," Chelsea said patiently.

"Well, perhaps so, dear," her mother replied, "but we don't associate with people like that."

Chelsea kissed her mother's cheek and started down the stairs. "We have to go, Mom."

Her mother hurried down the stairs after her. "Just remember, Chelsea, dear, that you're a well-brought-up young lady, won't you?"

"I will, Mom." Chelsea put her stuff in the back of the car, then got behind the wheel. Her mother got in the passenger seat.

"Because if you lie down with dogs, you get fleas," her mother added, clicking her seat belt in.

"Right," Chelsea said. "Dogs. Fleas."

"And you'll call me every night," her mother went on.

"If I can," Chelsea said absently, backing the car out of the driveway.

Her mother sighed, long and loud. "Well, it's only

a summer. In the fall you'll be right back here at home, safe and sound. You'll go to Vanderbilt with the right sorts of girls and boys, and you'll make lovely new friends. Won't that be nice?"

Chelsea didn't reply. Just the thought of living at home for college and going to Vanderbilt with "the right sort of girls and boys" felt like a noose tightening around her neck.

But maybe this summer will change everything, Chelsea thought as she pulled the car onto I-440 and hit the gas pedal. *Who knows? Maybe some miracle will occur and I won't have to come back here and go to Vanderbilt at all . . .*

She felt hopeful. And scared. And daring. And on the edge of a million possibilities.

Ready for New York. Ready for anything.

So long as no one found out who she really was.

"I'm coming, I'm coming. Keep your shirt on!" a nasal female voice with a definite New York accent called from inside the apartment.

From the other side of the door, Chelsea heard lock after lock turning, then a chain sliding, and finally the door opened, as the head of a very pretty Asian girl about Chelsea's age peeked out.

She had gorgeous long, straight black hair, and wore lots of black eyeliner and very pale lipstick.

"Yeah?" the girl said in a guarded voice. "You're—?"

"Chelsea Jennings," Chelsea said, picking up her suitcase. "One of the *Trash* interns? Didn't the doorman downstairs just announce me?"

"Yeah, like that means anything," the girl said. Now she opened the door completely, and Chelsea got a look at the rest of her. She was tiny, not much more than five feet tall, Chelsea figured. She wore ice-blue silk pants with a drawstring waist that fell below her navel and a matching cropped silk camisole.

The girl stepped aside and gestured Chelsea into the living room. "Honestly, you can't be too careful in this city. I'm Karma Kushner." She held out her hand for Chelsea to shake, then pointed at her. "Alicia Silverstone," she said.

"Pardon me?" Chelsea said.

"You look like that actress, Alicia Silverstone."

"Well, thanks," Chelsea said. "I mean, that's a nice compliment—"

"It's a thing I do," Karma said. "I look at people and decide what famous person they look most like. It drives my mother crazy. She looks like Anjelica Huston. 'Karma,' she always says, 'stop with the famous people look-alike bit!'"

"Your name is Karma—"

"Yeah, I know, it's bizarre," Karma agreed. "I mean, look at me, I'm Asian—I guess you noticed that—"

"Right off," Chelsea admitted.

"Yeah, right," Karma agreed. "And I have this, like, huggie-veggie first name and this Jewish last name, right? And, okay, I'm perfectly aware that I've got a voice like Fran Drescher on *The Nanny*, and you're like, 'what's up with that?' Am I right?"

"Kind of," Chelsea admitted.

"Jewish former-hippie parents," Karma explained. "I'm adopted. They own a New Age bookstore/health food store now, out on Long Island. They're still in mourning over the end of the Age of Aquarius. Meanwhile, I own twenty-three cashmere sweaters. I mean, they're, like, dying that they raised this materialistic daughter. So come on, I'll show you around."

She picked up Chelsea's suitcase—which was almost as big as she was—and carried it through the living room and down a long narrow hallway. Chelsea glanced into a bedroom and glimpsed a beautiful mahogany canopy bed and a bathroom with a shower curtain covered with nude Roman statues.

They turned into the third door on the right, a small furnished bedroom. The bedspread was bright pink, the bed was brass, the carpet was a worn oriental centered on a polished hardwood floor, and the wallpaper featured giant pink cabbage roses.

"I moved in two days ago," Karma said. "I couldn't wait to get out of Long Island. And, frankly, I took the best bedroom—with the canopy bed. This is the second best, if you can stomach Pepto-Bismol pink, which, frankly, is not one of my better colors. The other bedroom is tiny, but it has a water bed, in case you're into sex on the high seas."

"This is fine," Chelsea assured her. She felt both dazzled and a little shocked.

No one I know would talk about sex on a water bed, Chelsea thought.

Mom would just die, she added to herself gleefully.

"So, listen," Karma said. "You wanna come out and gab? Because I've been dying for company. Or you need to put your stuff away?"

"I can do that later," Chelsea said. "I didn't bring all that much anyway."

"Smart," Karma said. "Because the shopping in New York is to die for. I know every great discount place for designer clothes. Come on. I'll make coffee."

Chelsea followed Karma out of the room and went into the living room, while Karma went into the adjoining kitchen.

"I hope you like it really, really strong," Karma said, measuring out some coffee into Mr. Coffee.

"Truthfully, I usually drink tea," Chelsea said.

"Oh, gag me." Karma snorted. "Reminds me too much of my mom and dad. According to them, there's a tea for every occasion. Constipated? French verveine. Too aggressive? Camomile. Want to do past-life regression? There's a tea for it. Guaranteed."

Chelsea looked around the living room, trying to get acclimated. The furniture was old and substantial. She sat on a red velvet couch, shabby at the corners. A larger oriental rug than the one in her bedroom covered most of the floor. The tables were dark brown and the lace-covered lamps were old-fashioned.

Which made absolutely no sense when you looked at the artwork, which was modern, erotic, and—Chelsea thought—really, really bad.

"So, Chelsea, where are you from?" Karma asked as she got out two coffee cups. Clearly she had already learned where things were in the kitchen.

"Nashville, Tennessee," Chelsea replied. "You need help?"

"Nah," Karma said. "Yeah, you have a little accent. So you ever been to New York before?"

"Never," Chelsea said. "I've always dreamed about it. And now I'm finally here . . ." She stared at the painting behind the couch. It featured a naked woman standing on her head, balancing pianos on her feet. "The artwork in here is very strange," Chelsea said.

"It sucks," Karma said cheerfully, bringing in the coffee. "Can you believe how weird this apartment is? Old-lady furniture, and then a water bed in one bedroom and this *drek* on the walls?"

"I guess *Trash* rented it for us furnished," Chelsea said, sipping her coffee. She practically gagged, it was so strong.

"Yeah," Karma agreed. "But what I want to know is, who the hell furnished it?" She sat in the red velvet chair across from Chelsea and took a long swallow of her coffee.

"I live on this stuff," she continued. "I have this night job I just started—bartending at this club in the East Village—it's called Jimi's—after Jimi Hendrix, ya know? The guy who owns the place is named Arnold, which doesn't exactly ring a sexy bell, so I can see why he calls the place Jimi's." She took another sip of her coffee.

"Anyway," she continued, "I'm, like, doing a day job and a night job and I, like, live on caffeine. I should just do it intravenously!"

"Do you have to lie about your age to work there?" Chelsea asked. "Or are you older than eighteen—"

"Nah, I'm eighteen," Karma said. "I just graduated from South Long Island High School—that was three years of my life I'd sooner forget, thank you very much, but anyway, Jimi's is a teen club. No alcohol. They happen to be very hip at the moment. There's, like, this reverse thing happening with alcohol. It's really cool not to drink."

Chelsea nodded, as if all this information was normal to her. In actuality, her head was swimming and she felt overwhelmed. Clearly Karma loved to talk, though, so Chelsea didn't have to contribute too much for the time being.

"So, are you as psyched as I am about this *Trash*

thing?" Karma asked. "I couldn't believe it when they picked me!"

"Me neither," Chelsea agreed. "I mean, I feel like I'm so ordinary!"

"No one has ever described me as ordinary," Karma allowed, "but my grades in high school were so bad they barely let me graduate! I can't spell to save my life! God, I hope interns don't have to spell."

"You just use spell-check on the computer," Chelsea explained.

"Oh, yeah?" Karma said. "Great! Hey, you aren't one of those superbrains, are you?"

"Well, no—"

"Like one of those girls who got, like, fifteen hundred on her SATs—"

"No . . ." Chelsea said carefully.

Karma eyed her. "You got higher. I can tell."

"Well . . ."

"You did," Karma accused. "What did you get?"

"Fifteen-sixty," Chelsea admitted meekly. "But I'm just one of those people who tests well, and—"

"I'm dying here!" Karma whined. "Oh, my God, you are, like, *brilliant*!"

"Oh, I don't think I'm brilliant, I just—"

The buzzer next to the front door went off, loud and insistent.

"Our third roomie!" Karma cried, jumping up from her chair. "If she's another brain I'm killing myself." She pressed a black button on the wall and spoke into a small speaker. "Yeah?"

Static and noise came out of the speaker, followed by a garbled name neither girl could understand.

"Try again, Antoine," Karma called into the speaker.

More static and noise from the speaker.

"Yeah, sure, Antoine, have a nice day," Karma said into the speaker. "It could be a friggin' ax murderer and Antoine would send 'em up."

"He's the guy downstairs—?"

"Doorman," Karma said. "He stays up all night playing the trotters, he told me. Gonna hit it big and leave this job in the dust."

"Trotters?" Chelsea echoed.

"Yonkers Raceway? The horses? You got a lot to learn."

"And he actually told you that?" Chelsea asked.

"What can I say?" Karma whined. "People confide in me. Antoine suffers from serious sleep deprivation. And the intercom system is totally broken. Welcome to New York."

"Maybe we should report it to the manager of the building," Chelsea suggested. "And he'll see that it's fixed."

"Yeah, and maybe I'll find a Todd Oldham original at Woolworth's, but I doubt it," Karma said, draining her coffee.

Chelsea blushed and studied the bad art on the wall again while Karma took the coffee cups into the small kitchen. "Hey, do you cook?"

"Not much," Chelsea admitted.

"Me neither," Karma said. "Let's hope our third roomie is the Galloping Gourmet or we'll be living at the Greek diner on the corner."

The doorbell rang, and Karma went through her "who is it" routine through the door again. Of course the response was unintelligible, but Karma unlocked the locks, undid the chain and opened the door anyway.

"So, what we wanna know is, can you cook?" Karma asked the girl.

Chelsea couldn't see her since Karma was standing in front of the door.

"I can boil water," came a throaty reply, "but I only do it under duress."

"We're screwed," Karma said cheerfully, ushering the new girl into the apartment. "I'm Karma Kushner, by the way." She turned to look at Chelsea, pointing at the new girl. "Demi Moore," she pronounced, "but younger."

The new girl walked in and looked around, and Chelsea studied her. She had short, shaggy brown hair that fell sexily over her forehead into her large, almond-shaped blue eyes. She wore a pair of teeny, tiny cut-offs, a sleeveless black T-shirt, and black boots that laced almost up to her knees.

Chelsea could see the outline of a tattoo on her shoulder, though she couldn't make out what it was. The girl was utterly confident, curvy, sexy, and cool.

And totally intimidating.

All she carried was a shabby backpack, which she dropped in the center of the living room floor.

"Wow, weird," the girl said, looking around at the conservative furniture and the bad erotic art.

Something about her is familiar, Chelsea mused, *something about her voice . . .*

"What's with the tacky art?" the girl asked in her throaty, sexy voice, making a face at the upside-down nude.

"We wondered, too," Chelsea said.

And then, for the first time, the new girl looked at Chelsea. Really looked at her. She blinked slowly. "No," she said. "It can't be."

"Pardon me?" Chelsea asked, taken aback.

The new girl stared at her for another beat, and then she laughed.

"She's laughing," Karma commented as she shut the door. "I didn't hear a joke, but the girl clearly finds something hilarious."

"It's a pretty good joke, too," the girl said, her hands shoved into the tight pockets of her cut-offs. She looked right at Chelsea. "You don't recognize me?"

Chelsea studied her. "I'm sorry. I mean, if we've

met before, I guess I don't remember. Your voice sounds familiar, but—"

"It should," the girl said. She took a step towards Chelsea. "You're Chelsea."

Chelsea's heart thudded in her chest. *Oh, God, please don't let this be my worst nightmare come true,* she thought. *Please don't let this be someone who knows the truth about me. No, I'm being paranoid. No one knows. It can't be—*

"Chelsea," the girl said, taking her hands out of her pockets. "It's Alyssa."

Now it was Chelsea's turn to stare. Alyssa *Bishop?* Alyssa Bishop had been Chelsea's best friend all through grade school and junior high, but then she and her family had moved to Denver, and after about six months of letter writing, they had lost touch with one another.

But this can't be Alyssa. Alyssa was overweight, with an overbite that made her top teeth stick out. She was shy, quiet, and an excellent student, Chelsea thought.

But even if some kids thought Alyssa was kind of geeky, Chelsea knew how smart and funny and irreverent Alyssa really was, how she was the most fun person in the world to be with, how she could make anything exciting. She wasn't the lump her parents or the other kids thought she was at all. In fact, behind her thick glasses were the sparkling, mischievous blue eyes of—

Chelsea stared into the new girl's eyes.

Blue. So blue. Just like Alyssa's. And the voice, the funny, froggy, sexy voice that didn't seem to go with the plump, funny-looking young girl at all.

"Alyssa Bishop?" Chelsea whispered.

"It's really me," the girl said. "Only everyone calls me Lisha now."

"But . . . you changed," Chelsea managed.

Lisha laughed. "You didn't."

And the next thing they knew, they were hugging and laughing and crying, all at the same time.

"I love happy endings," Karma said, "but I feel like I missed the first reel of the movie here."

Chelsea broke away from Lisha, a huge grin on her face. "We were best friends when we were kids," Chelsea explained. "But Alyssa moved to Denver—"

"And I changed, thank God," Lisha added. "I used to be fat—"

"You?" Karma asked incredulously. "I would kill to have a body like yours. I practically have to buy my clothes in the children's department."

"Believe me, I was a lump," Lisha said. "And I had this overbite and glasses."

"But you were always wonderful," Chelsea said. "I missed you so much when you moved away . . . God, I just can't believe this!"

"Me either," Lisha said. She shook her head in

wonder. "This is really out there. What are the odds that the two of us would both get picked to be interns at *Trash*?"

"Slim to none," Chelsea said. She felt as if her mouth would break from smiling so hard. "I want to hear about everything that's happened to you!"

"Oh, this means I need to make more coffee," Karma said. "Hey, I hope you like water beds," she added to Lisha as she hurried into the kitchen.

"Depends on who's in it with me," Lisha said. She sat on the couch. So did Chelsea. "So, tell me—"

There was a knock on the door.

"Who's that?" Karma asked. "The doorman didn't buzz us."

Chelsea and Lisha just shrugged.

Another knock.

"We could buzz down to Antoine," Karma said. "Not that he'd be conscious enough to offer an opinion."

"Let's just open the door," Lisha said, getting up from the couch.

"Oh, sure," Karma said sarcastically, hurrying across the room. "And if any of us could cook we could invite Freddy Krueger out there to dinner. He'd supply the fresh meat."

She stood on tiptoe so she could see through the peephole in the door. "Who is it?" she yelled.

"Ick!" came a male voice.

"Okay, there's a guy standing at our door yelling 'ick.' I can't see a thing through the stupid peephole. What do we do?"

Lisha strode over to the door. "Who?" she called.

"Nick!" the voice yelled.

Karma shrugged. "So kill me. It sounded like 'ick' to me."

Lisha looked through the peephole. "There's more than one guy out there," she said. "In fact, it looks like three," she reported. "I'm opening the door."

"Are you on drugs?" Karma screeched. "This is New York! You can't just—"

The door was open. Chelsea and Karma both peered around Lisha to see who was there.

It was, as reported, three guys.

Three *cute* guys.

Three *incredibly* cute guys.

"Hi," said the one standing in the front with the Brad Pitt blue eyes and dirty-blond ponytail. "I'm Nick Shaw. This is Alan Van Cleef and Sky Addison," he added, cocking his head toward the two guys with him.

One had dark hair and a sensitive, finely chiseled face, and the other had short brown hair and the lean, muscular body of a serious athlete.

"We're the other three *Trash* interns," Nick explained. He smiled a dazzling smile.

"And we live right across the hall."

CHERIE BENNETT
BELIEVERS
F A N   C L U B

Hey, Readers! You asked for it, you've got it!

Join your Sunset sisters from all over the world in the greatest fan club in the world . . .

Cherie Bennett Believers Fan Club!

Here's what you'll get:

★ a personally-autographed-to-you 8 x 10 glossy photograph of your favorite writer (I hope!).
★ a bio that answers all those <u>weird questions</u> you always wanted to know, like how Jeff and I met!
★ a three-times yearly newsletter, telling you <u>everything</u> that's going on in the worlds of your fave books, and me!
★ a personally-autographed-by-me membership card.
★ an awesome bumper sticker; a locker magnet or mini-notepad.
★ "Sunset Sister" pen pal information that can hook you up with readers all over the world! Guys, too!
★ and much, much more!

So I say to you - don't delay! Fill out the request form here, clip it, and send it to the address below, and you'll be rushed fan club information and an enrollment form!

Yes! I'm a Cherie Bennett Believer! Cherie, send me information and an enrollment form so I can join the **CHERIE BENNETT BELIEVERS FAN CLUB!**

My Name _____

Address _____

Town _____

State/Province _____ Zip _____

Country _____

CHERIE BENNETT BELIEVERS FAN CLUB
P.O. Box 150326
Nashville, Tennessee 37215 USA

items offered may be changed without notice